# MANDIE
## AND THE
## MYSTERIOUS
## BELLS

# Mandie Mysteries

# MANDIE
## AND THE
# MYSTERIOUS
# BELLS

**Lois Gladys Leppard**

# BETHANY HOUSE PUBLISHERS
MINNEAPOLIS, MINNESOTA 55438
A Division of Bethany Fellowship, Inc.

*Mandie and the Mysterious Bells*

Lois Gladys Leppard

Library of Congress Catalog Card Number 87–72792

ISBN 1–55661–000–9

Published by Bethany House Publishers
A Division of Bethany Fellowship, Inc.
6820 Auto Club Road, Minneapolis, Minnesota 55438

Printed in the United States of America

With love
to my other granddaughter,
Jordan Leigh Leppard,
that adorable, brown-eyed dear,
who knows Mandie's story
but can't read it herself yet.

"Blessed are the merciful; for they shall obtain mercy."

St. Matthew 5:7

## About the Author

LOIS GLADYS LEPPARD has been a Federal Civil Service employee in various countries around the world. She makes her home in Greenville, South Carolina.

The stories of her own mother's childhood are the basis for many of the incidents incorporated in this series.

# Table of Contents

# Chapter 1 / Grandmother's Mystery

As Mandie stepped off the train with Jason Bond in Asheville, North Carolina, she found her good friend Celia waiting on the depot platform.

"Celia!" she exclaimed. "How did you get here?"

"Your grandmother sent me," Celia replied. The two girls embraced each other. "You see, she asked my mother to let me come back a day early for school on account of the mystery that she wrote you about."

Mandie pulled her coat around her more tightly to keep out the cold wind. "Has she told you what it's all about yet?" she asked eagerly.

"No, she's waiting for you," Celia answered. She turned to greet Mandie's companion. "How are you, Mr. Bond?"

"Fine, little lady," Mr. Bond replied, smiling down at the girl. "Mr. and Mrs. Shaw were busy, so they sent me with Miss Amanda."

"Come on," Celia urged. "Ben is waiting with the rig over there." She led the way down the platform. "Here he comes now. Have you got all your baggage?"

"I'll get the trunk, Missy," Mr. Bond offered, hurrying to where all the luggage had been unloaded from the train.

Ben drove the rig over to pick up the baggage, and

the two men loaded the trunk and the bag Mandie was carrying.

Ben smiled at Mandie. "Welcome home, Missy. We'se glad to have you back."

Mandie laughed. "Thanks, Ben, but my grandmother's house is not home," she reminded him. "My mother and stepfather, Uncle John, back in Franklin would have a fit if they heard you call this home."

"But you lives at dat Miz Heathwoods' school back up yonder on de hill . . ." Ben looked puzzled.

"Only while school is going on," Mandie explained as they climbed into the horse-drawn vehicle.

"Den you lives different places, don't you now?" Ben shook the reins and the horses started on their way.

"Yes, I suppose so—ever since I met up with Mr. Jason here at my Uncle John's house in Franklin," Mandie said, reaching over to squeeze Mr. Bond's hand. "He's my uncle's caretaker, you know. And he helps us solve our mysteries sometimes."

"Now, Miss Amanda . . ." Jason Bond laughed. "All I really do when you're at home is try to keep up with whatever you're into next."

Ben looked at Mr. Bond and winked. "Dat's impossible, Mistuh Bond," he said. "Impossible to keep up wid dese two girls."

Jason Bond smiled.

"Well, Ben, we have a brand new mystery," Mandie announced. "And as soon as my grandmother tells us about it, we'll get right to work on it." Her blue eyes sparkled as she talked. "Grandmother sent me a message to come back to school a day early so I could spend the night with her. She said something mysterious is going on here in Asheville."

Ben grinned. "Good luck!"

"I'm thankful I have to go back home tomorrow," Mr. Bond joked.

Mandie and Celia laughed.

Ben pulled the rig up in front of Mrs. Taft's huge mansion. The girls jumped down and ran to the door.

They found Mrs. Taft sitting in the parlor by the big open fireplace, where logs blazed and crackled their own welcome. As Mandie's grandmother rose to greet them, she smoothed her faded blonde hair. She was a tall woman, and very dignified except when she was helping her granddaughter solve mysteries.

Mandie gave her a big hug. "Tell us about the mystery, Grandmother!" she cried excitedly.

"Not until you get your coats off," Mrs. Taft replied. She turned to greet Mr. Bond, who had followed the girls into the room. "Thanks for bringing Amanda," she said.

"I was glad to do it, ma'am," Jason Bond said. "It sure feels good in here. It's gettin' purty cold out there now."

The two girls hastily removed their coats and hats and handed them to the maid who stood waiting. Mr. Bond gave the maid his coat, and she hung everything on the hall tree just outside the parlor doorway.

"I imagine it is cold out there," Mrs. Taft said. "Come on over by the fire." She turned to the maid. "Ella, we'll be ready for some hot coffee and cocoa when you finish there."

"Yes, ma'am," Ella answered from the doorway. "I'll git it right heah." She hurried on down the hallway.

"Do sit down, Mr. Bond," Mrs. Taft told the man, indicating the armchair opposite hers by the fireplace. "We'll have something to warm us up in a few minutes. Then in a little while the cook will have dinner ready."

Mr. Bond took the chair opposite Mrs. Taft as Mandie and Celia sat on footstools by the hearth.

"Where is Hilda?" Mandie asked.

"She's staying with the Smiths next door until y'all go back to school," Mrs. Taft replied. "I didn't want her involved in this adventure. You know how she is. She runs away every chance she gets, and I'm afraid one day we might not find her."

"You're a mighty good lady to give her a home," Mr. Bond remarked.

"Well, I had to," Mrs. Taft insisted. "I couldn't let her be put in some mental institution, especially since it was Mandie and Celia who found her hiding in the school attic."

"But she's getting better," Mandie reminded them. "Dr. Woodard said she is."

"Yes, she is," Mrs. Taft agreed.

"She's bound to improve now that her parents can't keep her shut up in a room like they did," Mr. Bond smiled.

"I think so too. But now, Grandmother, please tell us about the mystery—please!" Mandie begged, clasping her small white hands around her knees.

"Well, it's like this," her grandmother began. "There's something very mysterious going on here in Asheville. The bells on our church downtown have been ringing thirteen times at the stroke of midnight."

"Do they ring thirteen times at noon, too?" Mandie asked.

"No, just at midnight," her grandmother replied. "And no one can figure out what's wrong. The bells are activated by the clock on the hour and half past the hour. Several people have examined the bells and the clock mechanism, but they haven't found a thing wrong," she explained.

"Sounds spooky," Celia whispered.

"Some folks say it's a bad omen, and the whole town is upset because no one can solve the mystery." Mrs. Taft paused for a moment. "I know you girls are good at things like this, so I thought maybe you'd like to look into it."

"Sure, Grandmother," Mandie quickly agreed. "I think we could find out what's wrong. Don't you, Celia?"

"Well, we could try," Celia replied.

"We have almost all day today, and we don't have to check into school until tomorrow afternoon," Mandie said. "Grandmother, could we all just go down to the church and look around?"

"It's too cold out there for me, but if Mr. Bond would agree to escort you two girls, you may go after we eat," Mrs. Taft promised. "You'll have to bundle up, though. There's no heat in the church except when there's a service, you know."

"Mr. Jason, will you take us, please?" Mandie begged.

"I reckon I can go with you girls, long as you don't stay too long," he replied. "Like your grandmother said, it's cold out there for these old bones."

"Thanks," Mandie said, reaching over to squeeze his hand.

"How do we get inside?" Celia asked. "Who has the key?"

"It never is locked, dear," Mrs. Taft answered, "until the sexton makes his rounds about bedtime. Then he locks the doors. But he opens them again early every morning."

As Mrs. Taft finished speaking, the church bells rang in the distance. They all listened and counted.

Mandie pointed to the china clock on the mantelpiece. "That clock says it's eleven o'clock," she said, "but the bells rang twelve times. I counted."

"I did, too," Celia agreed.

"You're right," Mrs. Taft said. "So now the bells are not correct in the daytime either. Did you count the rings, Mr. Bond? Was it twelve?"

The old man nodded. "Yes, you're right. It was twelve. Maybe the clock mechanism needs repair."

"Several workmen have examined everything, but they found nothing wrong," Mrs. Taft repeated. "Of course, they didn't tear the clock apart, from what I understand, but they did inspect all the connections between the clock and the bells. There just doesn't seem to be anything wrong."

Ella the maid entered the room carrying a large silver tray with a steaming silver coffeepot and a silver teapot of hot cocoa. She set the tray on the low table by Mrs. Taft.

"I'll pour it, Ella. Thank you," Mrs. Taft said. "Would you let us know just as soon as dinner is ready?"

"Yes, ma'am," Ella replied, leaving the room.

"I know you girls like hot cocoa," Mrs. Taft said as she leaned forward to pour for them, "but what about you, Mr. Bond? Would you care for coffee or cocoa?"

"Coffee—black, please, ma'am," he answered. "Once I got old enough to drink coffee, I've never stopped. Guess you'd call me an old coffee sot," he laughed.

Mrs. Taft passed him a cup of steaming coffee, and then poured some for herself. "I suppose I am, too," she said, sipping the hot coffee. "However, once in a great while I get a taste for hot cocoa."

Mandie warmed her hands on her hot mug of cocoa and took a drink. "Grandmother, Joe said he would be here this weekend with his father," she said. "He promised to bring Snowball with them since they'll be coming in the buggy. I didn't want to bother with Snowball on the train."

"I knew they were coming," Grandmother acknowledged. "Dr. Woodard told me when I was at your house for Thanksgiving last week. And I knew they would bring that cat of yours." She smiled and took another sip of her coffee. "Now as soon as you girls finish your cocoa, run upstairs to your rooms and freshen up for dinner."

"Rooms?" Mandie questioned. "We only need one room, Grandmother."

"Well, I had Annie make up two rooms next to each other," Grandmother Taft explained, "but if you want to share one, that's all right. Just don't stay awake talking all night."

"We won't. Thanks," Mandie said. She and Celia quickly put their empty cups on the silver tray and jumped up. "We'll be back in a few minutes."

Grabbing their coats and bonnets from the hall tree, they headed upstairs.

The girls' baggage had been put in separate rooms, but the door between was standing open.

"I think I'll change into something more comfortable," Mandie called to Celia in the other room. She hung her coat and bonnet in the huge wardrobe.

"And warmer," Celia called back from the other room.

"I think I'll wear this." Mandie took an indigo woolen dress from the trunk and held it up for Celia to see through the doorway. "And I'll wear my wool cape with the hood so I don't have to wear a bonnet."

"Me, too," Celia said, holding up a dark green woolen dress. "And I'll wear this."

Mandie changed her clothes quickly. "Don't forget your boots," she reminded her friend.

Celia laughed. "You'd think we were going to the North Pole!"

"Well, it does seem awfully cold—a lot colder than it was at home," Mandie said. "Was it cold in Richmond?"

"I suppose so. I didn't really notice because I wasn't outdoors much, what little time I was there," Celia answered. "By the time I left your house after Thanksgiving and got home to Richmond, your grandmother had sent my mother a message asking if I could come back to school a day early and spend the night with her."

Celia finished dressing first and joined Mandie in her room. Sitting on the footstool by the warm fireplace, she straightened her stockings above the top of her shiny black boots.

"Just think," Mandie said as she shook down her long

skirt which partially covered her boots, "the year 1900 will soon be gone. Thanksgiving has passed and Christmas is coming up." She turned to the tall mirror standing nearby and smoothed the long blonde braid which hung down her back.

"Time sure does fly," Celia agreed. "We're almost halfway through our first year at the Heathwoods' school, but it seems like we just started a few weeks ago."

"Maybe that's because we seem to get so many holidays," Mandie laughed. "Pretty soon we'll be getting out for Christmas."

Celia grew quiet. "It'll be the first Christmas for both of us without our fathers, won't it?" she said softly.

Mandie nodded. "I remember Christmas morning last year back there in Swain County," she said. "My father had brought in a small Christmas tree and we had decorated it. I got up so early I caught him wrapping presents by the tree, but he just laughed and said it wasn't time to get up yet. I stayed up, though, and helped him finish." She blinked back tears in her blue eyes.

"Our whole family was at our house for Christmas last year," Celia recalled. "All my aunts, uncles, and cousins—everybody. They stayed for days and days." Her eyes brightened. "My father gave me my pony for Christmas." She smiled.

"I know y'all raise horses," Mandie said, approaching a touchy subject carefully, "and you said your father was killed when he was thrown from a horse. Was it a new horse, or had y'all had it a long time?"

"He had just bought it the day before." Celia's voice quivered. "Mother sold it after it threw my father."

"I guess I was lucky that my father didn't die so suddenly," Mandie conceded. "He got a bad cold that turned into pneumonia." She drew a long breath. "He died in April, right when the weather was turning warm and the wildflowers were beginning to bloom."

A light tap on the door made the girls look up. Mandie opened the door to find Annie, the upstairs maid, standing there.

"Miz Taft, she say fo' you girls to git downstairs. Dinnuh be on de table," Annie announced.

"Thanks, Annie," Mandie smiled. "We're coming right down." As the maid left, Mandie turned to Celia. "Guess we'd better get going."

"Yes, let's hurry so we can get through dinner and go down to the church," Celia agreed.

The girls rushed through the meal as fast as they could. Mrs. Taft and Mr. Bond seemed to be in no hurry. They sat talking and sipping coffee while Mandie and Celia squirmed in their seats.

When Ella came in to refill the coffee cups, Mrs. Taft smiled at the girls. "Ella," she said, "ask Ben to bring the rig around to the front door, please. These girls seem anxious to leave."

"Let us walk, please, Grandmother," Mandie begged. "It's not far."

Ella waited.

"No, it's too cold out there today," Mrs. Taft replied. "Besides, you forget that Mr. Bond's legs are not as young as yours." She looked up at the maid. "Go ahead, Ella, and tell Ben."

As the maid left the room, Mandie smiled at Jason Bond. "Sorry, Mr. Jason," she said. "I keep forgetting that you are older than we are."

Everyone laughed.

"A good bit older, young lady," Mr. Bond teased. "I know you're used to your old Indian friend, Uncle Ned, chasing around on adventures with you, but I'm just too old for that—or maybe I should say too old and too lazy."

Mandie smiled across the table at him. "We love you anyhow, Mr. Jason."

"You girls may be excused." Mrs. Taft looked amused.

"Wrap up good now," she called as they hurried from the room.

Taking the steps two at a time, they stopped in their rooms only long enough to snatch up their cloaks and gloves. Mr. Bond buttoned up his warm coat and waited in the front hallway.

When they were all in the rig, Ben shook the reins and sent the horses flying. The girls squealed with delight and held on tightly. Jason Bond looked from them to Ben but didn't say a word.

Ben grinned broadly. "I loves to go fast," he explained, "but Miz Taft, she don't like it, so I'se glad to have some fun and git y'all to the church quick."

Mandie and Celia laughed, but Jason Bond just held on and looked straight ahead.

After a few minutes Ben pulled the horses up sharply in front of the big brick church and everyone lurched. Ben grinned again.

"Thanks, Ben," Mandie said, scrambling down from the rig with Celia and Mr. Bond close behind. "I guess you did get us to the church quick. That was fun!"

"Yeh, Missy," the Negro man replied. "Now, is I s'posed to wait heah or come back latuh to git y'all?"

Mr. Bond spoke up. "You'd better wait here, Ben," he said. "We won't be inside very long. You can come inside with us if you think it's too cold to sit out here."

"I be all right out heah," Ben replied, settling back in his seat.

The girls and Mr. Bond stopped to stare up at the tall steeple where the huge clock was mounted. They could faintly see the bells inside the belfry.

"Looks normal," Mr. Bond remarked.

"But it's—" The bells interrupted Mandie to ring once for one o'clock. "Well, it rang right this time," she said.

"Must be something wrong inside," Celia suggested

as they started up the wide steps to the double front doors on the porch of the church.

Mr. Bond stepped ahead of the girls to open the door for them and ushered them inside.

Mandie looked around the familiar sanctuary. "This is where we go to church while we're at the Heathwoods' school, Mr. Bond," she said. "Grandmother Taft is a member here."

"Sure is a big church," the old man commented as he walked around.

"Let's go up in the gallery," Mandie suggested.

"I'll stay down here," Mr. Bond said, sitting down in a nearby pew. "Just don't get into anything up there now."

"Come on, Celia!" Mandie led the way to a door at the back of the church. Opening the door, she started up the steps to the gallery, and Celia followed.

At the top of the stairs, Mandie surveyed the rows and rows of benches. "I've never been up here before," she said.

"I don't see any bells. How do we get to them?" Celia asked.

As the girls looked around, they spotted another door at the end of the gallery. They hurried over to open it. There, high above their heads, hung the huge bells in the belfry. Heavy ropes dangled down in various places.

"How can we get up there?" Mandie asked. "There aren't any steps going up to the bells."

"It looks awfully high from down here," Celia noted.

Mandie touched the ropes carefully for fear she would cause the bells to ring. Then she saw that some of the rope was actually a rope ladder extending up into the belfry. "Here!" she exclaimed, shaking the rope. "We have to go up this ladder."

Celia looked at the rope in fright. "Go up a rope ladder? We can't do that, Mandie."

"Yes, we can," Mandie assured her. "It won't be any

worse than walking over a swinging bridge, and I've done that lots of times without falling."

"But I've never been on a swinging bridge," Celia protested. "That thing will swing around and we could fall off."

"We won't if we're careful to hold on real tight," Mandie said. Quickly removing her cape and gloves, she threw them on a nearby bench and grasped the first rung of the rope ladder. "Come on."

Celia slowly removed her cape as she stood watching. "I'll get all dizzy and fall," she argued.

"No you won't," Mandie assured her. "Just don't look down. Keep looking up. Come on." She swung onto the next rung of the ladder and began to make her way up.

Celia nervously watched the ladder swing with Mandie's weight. She didn't move.

Reaching the top, Mandie stepped into the belfry and looked around at the huge bells. "Come on, Celia. You can see the whole town from up here," she called down to her friend. "You won't fall if you hold on with all your might. Come on."

"Well, all right. I'll try," Celia finally agreed. As she reached up and grasped the first rung of the ladder, it swung around and she stopped. Her heart beat wildly and her hands grew clammy.

Mandie knelt down on the floor of the belfry at the top of the ladder. "Reach up for the next rung, Celia," she called. "Keep looking up. Don't look down."

Celia took a deep breath and did what her friend said. Slowly, carefully, she made her way up the ropes. After several minutes she grasped the top rung and started to reach for Mandie's extended hand, but then she looked down. "Oh!" she gasped, shaking with fright. "Look how far it is down to the floor!"

Mandie grabbed Celia's hand and gave her such a hard pull that Celia sprawled onto the floor of the belfry beside her.

Celia closed her eyes. "I just know I'll never make it back down," she moaned.

"Come on. Get up," Mandie said, helping her to her feet. "Look outside. You can see everywhere from up here."

There were rafters running every which way. The only floor to walk on was a small piece supporting the bells, and a narrow walkway around the outer edge of the belfry. Celia held onto Mandie's hand as they carefully made their way around the narrow walkway to peer outside at the town.

"I thought you were the one who got dizzy-headed from heights," Celia reminded Mandie. "Remember telling me about the widow's walk at Tommy's house in Charleston?"

"But that was completely outside where if you slipped, you could fall all the way down to the ground," Mandie explained. "Up here we have these walls to protect us." She pointed down to the road. "Look, there's Ben in the rig down there."

Celia quickly turned back to look at the huge bells. "Let's get this exploration over with," she begged. "Just what are we looking for anyway?"

"Anything we can find," Mandie replied. As she stepped back over to the bells, Celia followed slowly and carefully.

Mandie's eyes searched the walls of the belfry. "Where are the connections to the clock?" she wondered aloud. "Where is the clock located from here?"

"Do you think the clock on the outside is as far up as the bells are?" Celia asked. "The clock is on the front side, remember?"

Mandie turned back to the front of the belfry. "No, I believe the clock is lower than the bells."

Celia found some wires and ropes coming out of the front wall. "Here it is!" she exclaimed. "The clock is on the outside of these wires and things. See? They go on over to the bells."

"You're right," Mandie agreed, carefully moving over to examine what Celia had found.

"But how does the clock make the bells ring, Mandie?" Celia asked.

"Well, I guess it's sort of like that big grandfather clock that my grandmother has. The pendulum trips something inside the clock and makes it chime," Mandie explained, tracing the wires.

"But how does the clock know how many times to strike?" Celia was baffled.

"Oh, Celia, I don't know everything," Mandie fussed as she traced the wires. "It just does somehow. The insides are made with one notch, two notches, or whatever, I suppose, to allow the clock to strike as it rotates—or something. Anyhow, these wires do go to the bells. See?"

Celia watched as Mandie followed the length of the wires to the bells. "I don't see anything wrong with them, do you?" she asked.

"No, they're all connected," Mandie replied.

Suddenly the girls felt the floor beneath their feet tremble slightly. Then there was a hard thud from somewhere below. They grabbed each other's hand.

"What was that?" Celia gasped.

"The whole place shook!" Mandie exclaimed.

"I think we'd better go back down," Celia decided.

"Yes, I suppose we'd better for now," Mandie agreed. "But we'll have to come back later. You go down the ladder first."

Celia sat down on the floor to grasp the rope ladder swinging below. After a few tries she finally got into a position to slide down onto the first rung. She held her breath and looked up at Mandie.

"Now don't look down," Mandie cautioned her from above.

At that moment one of Celia's hands missed a rung, and she grasped wildly into the air. Her hand found a rope hanging down from above. She grabbed it and hung on with all her might. Suddenly the bells started ringing. She was so frightened she slid down the rope and landed in a heap on the floor below. When she let go, the bells stopped ringing.

"Oh, Celia, are you all right?" Mandie called to her as she quickly came down to her. "I guess that rope is there to ring the bells by hand."

"At least it gave me some way to get down," Celia answered, trying to get her breath.

Just then they heard Mr. Bond's voice. "What are you girls doing up there?" he called from below. "I think you'd better get down here fast."

"We're coming," Mandie called back.

They grabbed their cloaks and gloves, and scurried around the gallery to the steps leading down into the sanctuary.

"We still don't know what was shaking everything or what that noise was," Celia reminded her friend as they reached the bottom of the stairs.

"I know, but we'll come back and find out," Mandie promised. "Anyway, we know what everything looks like up there now. Maybe Joe can help us when he gets here this weekend."

Mr. Bond was waiting for them at the bottom of the steps. "You know you'll have the whole town here in a minute, ringing those bells that way," he scolded. "What on earth were you doing up there?"

"I'm sorry, Mr. Bond," Celia apologized. "It was my fault. I slipped on the ladder and caught hold of the extra rope. I didn't know it would ring the bells."

"What ladder?" Mr. Bond wanted to know.

Celia glanced at Mandie. "The ladder to the belfry," she answered slowly.

"Now don't you girls go climbing any more ladders while you're in my care," the old man said. "Let's go outside and get going."

"Thanks for coming with us, Mr. Jason," Mandie said as they stepped into the rig where Ben was waiting.

Ben shook the reins, and the horses started off. "Did y'all find out whut makin' dem bells ring de wrong number at de wrong time?" he asked.

"No, but we will," Mandie promised.

"You hope," Celia whispered to her friend.

As they sped around the corner in the rig, the bells on the church rang three times. Everyone looked at each other.

"They rang three times, but it is really two o'clock," Celia said.

"I have an idea someone went up there as soon as we left," Mandie whispered.

"Thank goodness they didn't come up there *while* we were there," Celia replied.

"But we might have caught them if they had," Mandie reminded her.

## Chapter 2 / Strangers in the Church

Mandie and Celia were awake before daylight the next morning, excited because Mrs. Taft had promised them they could go back to the church. They lay there in the warm bed discussing the mystery of the bells. The wind was blowing cold and hard outside and rattling the shutters. Annie had not yet come to start the fire in the fireplace in the room. "What are we going to do this time when we go to the church?" Celia asked.

"I thought we could just stay there a while and watch to see if anyone comes into the church, especially when the clock strikes twelve noon," Mandie replied, pushing up her pillow so she could sit up in bed.

Celia did likewise and the two tugged at the heavy quilts to cover their shoulders.

"But if somebody comes into the church, what will we do?" Celia asked.

"We won't let them see us," Mandie replied. "We'll just hide somewhere where *they* can't see us but *we* can see them."

"That'll be hard to do in that big church," Celia noted. "It's so wide open."

"There are draperies on each side of the place where the choir sits, and there's a low short curtain that runs across the platform behind where the preacher stands.

The pews are so tall we might be able to hide between some of them, too," Mandie suggested.

"Well, what do we do if someone does come in?"

"We'll wait to see what they do, and then we'll just come out and ask them who they are, I suppose," Mandie answered.

"I sure hope no criminals come into the church while we're there." The way the bed was placed in the room the girls were facing the door directly. Celia was looking that way when the door softly and slowly came open. She moved closer to Mandie and gasped. As Annie appeared through the doorway, Mandie laughed and said, "It's Annie."

"Mornin', Missies," Annie greeted them as she went over to the fireplace. "Y'all awake nice and early. I'll jes' git dis heah fire goin' now, and it'll be warm in heah in no time, it will."

"Thanks, Annie," Mandie said. "It is cold in here."

The maid quickly cleaned out the ashes and put them in the bucket on the hearth. Then, after laying kindling for a new fire, she took a match from the pocket of her long white apron and lit the wood. The fire spread quickly and the logs crackled.

"I heard my grandmother tell my mother that she was going to have that steam heat put in, Annie," Mandie said. "You know, the kind of heat that you just turn a knob on this thing standing in the room and the heat comes right out. Then you won't have to build fires in the fireplaces anymore."

"Steam heat? Whut kinda heat be dat, Missy?" Annie stooped and fanned the fire with her apron to make it burn better.

"Like they have in Edwards' Dry Goods Store downtown," Mandie replied. "You know how warm it always is in there."

"Oh, you mean dem big hot metal things whut stand

up on de floor?" Annie rose from the hearth. "Well, dey ain't 'zackly magic. Dey gotta have a fire goin' some-wheres to make 'em git hot."

"I know," Mandie agreed, sliding out of bed and reaching for her slippers. "But I think it's just one big fire that makes them hot, probably in the basement, so you'd have only one fire to tend to." She hurried to stand in front of the warm fireplace as she quickly put on her robe.

Celia followed. "That's the kind of heat we have at home," she said, wrapping her robe around her. "Just about everybody in Richmond has that kind of heat now, but I don't know for sure how it works."

"Well, right now we ain't got it," Annie said, turning to leave the room, "so I'se got to go build more fires."

"Don't forget, Annie. Grandmother said you could go with us to the church this morning," Mandie reminded her.

"Lawsy mercy, Missy," Annie sighed. "I don't be knowin' why y'all wants to go traipsin' down to dat spooky church. Dem spooks down there is liable to git us."

"Oh, Annie, there's no such things as spooks," Mandie replied, smiling. "You wait and see. All that trouble with the bells is being caused by some good, solid human being—not something you can't catch hold of."

"Well, I sho' hopes dem bad human bein's don't git ahold of us," Annie mumbled as she went out the door.

"I do believe Annie is afraid to go with us," Mandie said, laughing as she and Celia sat on the rug by the fire.

"But, Mandie, it could be something—or someone—we *should* be afraid of," Celia reminded her.

At that moment the girls heard the church bells ringing in the distance. Silently, they counted to seven, and looked at the clock on the mantel.

"Right that time," Mandie said.

"Maybe they'll quit acting crazy and ring right all the time," Celia said.

"But then we wouldn't have a mystery to solve," Mandie argued. "I'm getting hungry. Let's get dressed and go find some breakfast."

After a delicious, hot breakfast, the girls were allowed to go to the church. Ben brought the rig around to the front door, and they were soon on their way.

The wind was still blowing hard and cold. The few people they saw walking on the streets were bundled up in heavy winter clothes. Winter had arrived.

Ben coaxed the horses to a fast speed, and Annie held onto her seat in fright.

"Now, you listen heah, you, Ben," she said sternly. "Don't you go runnin' wild like dat. You liable to git us all killed."

"But de Missies, dey like ridin' fast, don't you now?" he called back to the girls.

"Not too fast, please, Ben," Celia replied.

"We don't want to scare Annie, so would you please slow down a little, Ben?" Mandie asked.

"All righty, Missy. We sho' don't wanta skeer dis old woman up heah beside me, does we now?" Ben replied, laughing as he slowed the horses.

Annie twisted around and gave Ben a mean look. "Whut old woman?" she demanded. "Ain't me. I ain't old as you are. Won't be eighteen 'til next summer."

"Well, if you ain't old, den quit actin' like you wuz," Ben replied. As he pulled the rig up in front of the church, he turned to grin at the girls. "Heah we be's," he announced.

The girls jumped down from the rig and waited for Annie. She looked back at Ben. "Ain't you comin' wid us?"

"I stays right heah," Ben replied, settling back comfortably in the driver's seat.

"He can't go in with us, Annie," Mandie told the maid.

"That would be too many people to hide. There are three of us already. Come on."

As they entered the church, they looked around. There was no one in the vestibule or the sanctuary.

"Annie, we have to hide you somewhere," Mandie said, walking toward the altar. "How about standing behind those draperies up there where the choir sits?"

"Lawsy mercy, Missy. Why I got to hide?" Annie asked nervously.

"We came here to watch to see if anyone goes up there and rings the bells. We all have to hide," Mandie explained. "Come on. You can get behind those draperies. It'll be more comfortable than sitting down on the floor behind that low curtain across the platform like we're going to do."

Annie reluctantly followed Mandie and Celia to the draperies. The girls showed her how to keep herself hidden. There was even a small stool back there where she could just barely have room to sit.

The girls stepped back to look at the dark red plush draperies as they fell into folds and concealed Annie.

"Just right," Celia remarked.

"Annie, please don't make any noise or come out unless we come back there to get you," Mandie warned.

"I sho' won't, Missy. Jes' you don't fo'git and leave me heah all day," Annie answered from behind the draperies.

"We won't. We're only going to stay until the bells ring at twelve noon. Then we have to go back and get ready to check into school," Mandie explained.

The girls hurried over to the low curtain across the platform behind the pulpit. They stepped behind it and sat down on the floor.

Celia looked at the curtain in front of her, which was only a little higher than her head. "It just barely hides us," she said.

"We can peek through the holes where the curtain

rings are, though. See?" Mandie said, bending forward to fit her eye to the opening for the rod. "Mandie! I just thought of something!" Celia said suddenly. "We forgot to look up in the gallery and the belfry to see if anyone was already up there."

Mandie sprang to her feet. "You're right," she said. "We need to be sure there's no one there. Let's go see."

They dropped their capes and gloves behind the curtain where they had been hiding, and started for the stairs.

"Where you two gwine now?" Annie called from behind the draperies.

"We're just going to look upstairs, Annie. We'll be right back." Mandie answered. "Please stay where you are."

"I ain't stayin' heah long by myself," Annie called back.

"We'll be back in a minute," Mandie promised.

The girls hurried to the door and raced up the stairs to the gallery. No one was there. They opened the door to look up into the belfry. No one was there, either.

"We can't see inside the whole belfry from down here," Mandie said, moving around to look upward. She grabbed the end of the rope ladder. "You stay right here. I'm going up there to look around."

"Be careful," Celia whispered, as Mandie quickly climbed up the rope ladder.

At the top Mandie walked around. "Nobody up here, either," she called. She quickly came back down the swinging rope ladder. As she let go of the last rung, she sat down hard on the floor.

"Are you all right?" Celia bent down to make sure her friend wasn't hurt.

"I'm all right," Mandie assured her. "I came down too fast, and it made the ladder swing too much. I just let go to keep from swinging around." She stood up and brushed off her skirt.

The girls again took up their watch behind the low curtains. They sat still and talked only in whispers in case someone suddenly came into the church. During a long silence, the girls were startled when Annie sneezed loudly.

"Bless you," Celia called to the maid.

"I hope you're not getting a cold, Annie," Mandie said in a loud whisper.

"I ain't got no cold yet, but I will have if I has to stay in dis cold place much longer," Annie complained. Suddenly the draperies moved, there was a loud crash, and the Negro girl fell through the opening in the draperies.

Mandie and Celia jumped up and ran to her rescue.

"I be all right." Annie got up from the floor. "Dis dad-blasted stool jes' turned over. Dat's all." She set the stool upright again. "Y'all go on back and git dis over wid so's we kin go home." She returned to her hiding place.

Mandie and Celia resumed their watch from behind the low curtains.

"It won't be long till twelve o'clock, Annie," Mandie called.

She and Celia put their capes around themselves and huddled together. It was cold in the church.

Before long the huge double doors of the church made a loud squeaking noise.

"Sh-h!" Mandie whispered.

As she and Celia peered through the holes in the curtain, an expensively dressed woman appeared inside the sanctuary. A tall, neatly attired man followed her from the vestibule down the center aisle.

Mandie's heart did flipflops as she watched and waited. Celia grabbed Mandie's hand tightly.

The couple talked in low voices as they walked down the aisle, pausing to look into each pew on both sides, making their way toward the front.

Mandie strained her ears but couldn't make out what the strangers were saying. She just hoped Annie would stay out of sight.

As the strangers neared the altar, Mandie could hear

a little of what they were saying.

"I know it's got to be here," the woman said. "I was . . ."

Mandie couldn't hear the end of the sentence because the woman had leaned down between the pews.

"Well, we have to find it," the man said firmly. "If someone else finds it, that wouldn't be too good."

"Oh, dear," the woman sighed. She seemed almost in tears.

"We've got to find it," the man repeated. "You go up that aisle over there, and I'll take this one over here." He indicated the two aisles at the sides of the church.

The woman started looking in the pews on the left as the man went to the right. "If only you'd stop blaming me," she moaned.

"I know it wasn't intentional, but it was your fault," the man told the woman. "If you hadn't decided to come into this church to keep from being seen you wouldn't have lost it."

"You told me to hide and I didn't know what else to do," the woman protested.

"Well, if you had stayed in one place instead of walking around looking at all those stained glass windows we'd know what area to search," he said. "It could be almost anywhere in here."

"I was afraid someone would come in and see me if I just sat still," the woman said. As the strangers got farther away up the aisles, Mandie couldn't make out what they were saying, but by the time they reached the back of the church, they were obviously arguing.

The man took the woman's arm and pointed to the last pew. She pulled her arm away and slid into the pew. But when the man sat down next to her, she moved away from him. Then taking a handkerchief from her purse, she dabbed at her eyes.

Mandie and Celia looked at each other. They dared

not even whisper for fear of being heard. The man seemed so angry, and the woman seemed to be afraid of him. The man was doing most of the talking. Oh, how the girls wished they could hear their conversation!

Finally, the strangers got up and started back down the outside aisles. This time they moved slower, carefully bending to look at the seat of each pew and then stooping to look beneath each one. They finally met in front.

"Nothing," the woman sobbed.

"Nothing over there, either. Let's go up this center aisle once more," the man said. "And please be sure you look very carefully."

As they walked along together, the woman took the left side and the man, the right. Once in a while the man would watch the woman when she wasn't looking as though he wanted to be sure of what she was doing.

Mandie realized her foot had gone to sleep from being cramped up behind the curtain, but she dared not change positions.

Celia shivered again and wrapped her arms about herself.

The strangers finally met at the back of the church, but just as the man opened his mouth to speak, the bells started ringing in the belfry. The man grabbed the woman by the arm and pushed her ahead of him as they rushed out the doors of the church.

Mandie and Celia sat stunned for a moment, looking at each other and mouthing the numbers as the bells rang—one, two, three ... Finally Mandie jumped up, stomping the foot that had gone to sleep, and hurriedly limped toward the stairs to the gallery. "Let's see who's in the belfry," she said.

Celia didn't seem in a hurry to run into someone up there, but she followed anyway.

As they ran up the stairs, they kept counting—out loud now. Across the gallery, they jerked open the door to the belfry.

"I'll go first," Mandie offered, grabbing the rope.

"You're not really going up there, are you?" Celia's voice quivered.

"Of course," Mandie called back.

The bells stopped after twelve rings and then sounded a weak, shaky thirteenth ring.

Mandie hurried up the ladder as Celia stood below and watched. She put her head through the opening at the top, and looked around before she got off the ladder. "There's nobody up here," she called, climbing onto the belfry floor. "I don't see a thing."

"Come on back down then," Celia hollered.

Then suddenly Mandie heard her name, "M-M-Mandie!" She looked down to see Celia frozen on the spot and white as a sheet.

A hand reached out and touched Celia on the shoulder. Celia screamed.

"Look behind you, Celia," Mandie yelled. "It's only Annie."

Trembling all over, Celia turned slightly.

Annie came around her and apologized. "I'se sorry, Missy," she said. "I didn't mean to skeer you. Y'all went and left me alone down there, and *I* jes' got skeered."

"Th-that's all right, Annie," Celia managed to say.

Annie looked up into the belfry just as Mandie hurried down the rope ladder. The hem of Mandie's long skirt was tucked into her waistband to keep it out of her way.

As Mandie swung onto the floor and straightened her skirt, Annie gasped. "Lawsy mercy, Missy. Miz Taft have a heart 'tack if she know you go climbin' round dat way."

"You worry too much, Annie," Mandie said. She turned to Celia. "Are you all right?"

Celia took a deep breath. "I am now," she said, her voice still trembling. "But I was sure whoever has been messing with the bells had caught me."

"I'm sorry, Celia," Mandie said. "I guess we'd better

go now. We have to get to school, you know."

"Thank goodness!" Celia exclaimed.

The three made their way through the gallery to the stairs.

"I didn't see anything going on up there, but there's got to be something wrong somewhere," Mandie said.

At the bottom of the stairs, Celia stopped. "And those people who were here a while ago," she said, "I wonder who they were and what they were looking for."

"I do, too," Mandie said as they went on through the vestibule. "Have you ever seen them before, Annie?"

"Now, Missy, jes' 'cause I lives in Asheville ain't no sign I knows ev'rybody in town," Annie said, opening the front door. " 'Sides, dis be white folks' church. I goes to my own church. I don't mix wid no white folks."

Mandie and Celia looked at each other and smiled as they went on down the front steps. Ben was waiting in the rig. He saw them coming and stepped down to the road by the rig.

"Not only dat," Annie continued, "dat lady didn't look like she come from dis heah town."

"What makes you say that?" Mandie asked.

"She jes' look too high uppity," Annie replied. "You know, too fancy dressed."

"Aren't there any fancy, uppity people in this town?" Mandie teased.

"No, not de likes of huh," Annie shook her head. "I don't think she live in dis heah town."

Mandie turned to Celia. "Why don't we look around outside while we're here?"

"We should go back to your grandmother's, shouldn't we?" Celia reminded her friend.

"Ben can walk with us if you're afraid we might find somebody," Mandie suggested. Without waiting for Celia's reply, she called the Negro man, "Ben, would you walk around the church with us?"

Ben walked over to them with a puzzled look on his face. "Why, 'course, Missy."

"Dat man couldn't catch nobody fo' you," Annie said with a teasing glance at the driver. "He too slow, dat Ben is."

Ben scowled at her. "Fust you says I'm too fast, and now you says I'm too slow," he grumbled. "Woman, make yo' mind up, or ain't you got one?"

Annie ignored him and walked on around the side of the church. The girls grinned at Ben and followed the Negro girl around the building.

Thick shrubbery grew against the church, but since it was wintertime, there weren't any leaves, and they could see right through the bushes. Annie stayed ahead of the other two girls, and Ben lagged behind as they all carefully looked over the outside of the building and the yard.

When they turned the back corner and faced the rear of the church, the girls stopped in amazement then ran up to the wall. There, all over the brick, was a lot of huge, illegible handwriting, evidently written with whitewash.

"What does it say?" Celia gasped.

"I cain't read dat," Annie fussed.

Ben stared at the writing with the others. "You cain't read nohow," he mumbled.

"I don't think it says anything," Mandie decided. She brushed her hand over the mess. "It's dry now, but it either dripped and ran together, or whoever wrote it didn't know how to write."

"Who in the world could have done such a thing? Imagine messing up a church building with all that!" Celia said.

"It's probably connected with the mystery of the bells," Mandie replied.

"Missy, I think we better git goin'," Annie spoke up.

"Let's just walk the rest of the way around the building," Mandie urged. "We can hurry."

She led the way. They returned to the front of the church without finding anything else unusual.

The girls were puzzled. What was that mess supposed to be? A message? A warning? And when did it get there? No one had mentioned that strange writing before.

The mystery was deepening.

# Chapter 3 / April's Threat

Later that day Ben loaded the luggage and drove the girls to school. As they rode up the half-circle graveled driveway, the huge, white clapboard house at the top of the hill came into view. Gray curls of smoke rose out of the tall chimneys. The giant magnolia trees surrounding the school were now bare.

The rig came to a halt in front of the long, two-story porch supported by six huge, white pillars. A small sign to the left of the heavy double doors read *The Misses Heathwood's School for Girls*. Tall narrow windows trimmed with stained glass flanked each side of the doors. Above the doors, matching stained glass edged a fan-shaped transom of glass panes.

The white rocking chairs, with their bare cane bottoms, were still sitting along the veranda behind the banisters. The green flowered cushions had been removed and taken inside for the winter. The wooden swing hung bleakly on its chains attached to the ceiling. Uncle Cal, the old Negro man who worked for the school, came out to help unload the baggage.

"Hello, Uncle Cal," Mandie greeted him as she and Celia stepped down from the rig. "Did you and Aunt Phoebe have a nice Thanksgiving?"

"Sho' did, Missy 'Manda, but we'se glad to see you

back," the old man replied. "You, too, Missy," he told Celia.

"Thanks, Uncle Cal," Celia replied, tossing back her long auburn hair. "Guess what! We have another mystery to solve."

" 'Nuther mystery? I sho' hope y'all ain't aimin' to git in no mo' trouble," the old man said, reaching for a bag in the rig.

"It's about the bells in the church downtown, Uncle Cal," Mandie explained. "They're ringing the wrong time."

"Ev'rybody know dat, Missy 'Manda. De whole town mad 'bout it. Cain't set no clock by dem bells no mo'." Uncle Cal turned to go up the front steps and Ben and the girls followed.

Celia laid her hand on Mandie's arm, and stopped her on the porch for a moment. Uncle Cal and Ben went inside with the luggage. "Mandie, I just remembered something," she said. "Remember what April Snow told us when we left school for the Thanksgiving holidays?"

"She said, 'Enjoy your holidays because you might not enjoy coming back,' wasn't that it?" Mandie asked.

"Her exact words," Celia confirmed. "What do you think she's planning to stir up now?"

"I have no idea, but we'll be on the lookout for her this time," Mandie assured her friend. "We'll be prepared."

They went on through the double doors into the long center hallway. They stopped and looked around the wainscoted, wallpapered hallway. It was empty. Their eyes traveled up the curved staircase leading to a second-story balcony, which ran near a huge crystal chandelier. The place seemed to be deserted.

They walked on. A tall, elderly lady with faded reddish-blonde hair, wearing a simple black dress, came out of the office off the hallway.

"Hello, Miss Hope," Mandie said, hurrying to greet the lady.

"I hope you girls had a nice holiday," Miss Hope Heathwood replied, putting an arm around each girl.

"We did, Miss Hope. I know y'all did, too, with all of us noisy girls gone," Celia said, laughing.

"Oh, but we missed you lively young ladies," Miss Hope said. "You know we only had three girls here over the holidays—just the ones who lived too far away to go home. But we hardly saw them. They would show up for meal time and then disappear for the rest of the day."

"April Snow didn't go home, did she?" Mandie asked.

"No. She's around somewhere," Miss Hope said. "Now y'all get upstairs and get unpacked before time for supper." She turned back toward the office.

"Yes, ma'am," the girls replied together.

Mandie and Celia hurried upstairs to their room. They had been lucky enough to get a small bedroom together near the stairs to the attic and the servants' stairway going down. The other girls lived in rooms with four double beds and eight girls in each. Even though Mandie and Celia's room was hardly more than a large closet that could barely accommodate the necessary furniture, they were happy there.

A fire in the small fireplace warmed the room. Uncle Cal and Ben had brought up their luggage. The girls hurriedly began unpacking their trunks.

"I want to make sure that whoever wrote on the church walls is punished to the limits of the law. No one should be allowed to treat the Lord's house that way," Mandie said. "It must have been done recently because Grandmother didn't know about it until we told her. And she always knows everything first."

"It was probably done while we were inside the church," Celia said.

"Maybe." Mandie shook out her dresses from the trunk and prepared to hang them in the huge chifforobe. With her hands full of clothes, she opened the door to the chifforobe.

A small mouse quickly jumped out, landing on her boot and causing her to drop everything.

"A mouse! Look out!" Mandie screamed.

The mouse frantically ran around in circles on the carpet, apparently looking for a way to hide.

"I'll get Uncle Cal!" Celia yelled. She almost knocked down Aunt Phoebe as she ran out the door.

The old Negro woman appeared in the doorway with a broom, and found Mandie standing up on the bed, too frightened to move.

"I wuz jes' sweepin' de hall when I hears Missy scream," Aunt Phoebe said. "Lawsy mercy, whut be de matter?"

"A mouse, Aunt Phoebe!" Mandie cried.

"It c-came out of the ch-chifforobe," Celia stuttered, watching the floor around her feet for the creature.

"I don't see no mouse, Missy. Where it be?" Aunt Phoebe asked, sweeping the broom around the room. "I don't see none. It must be done gone and hid now."

"I d-don't know, Aunt Phoebe," Mandie said, collapsing on the bed.

Aunt Phoebe picked up the clothes Mandie had dropped in a pile and laid them on a chair. She examined the chifforobe. "I don't see how no mouse could git in there," she said. "Ain't no holes or cracks in it." She closed the door to see how it fit. "Somebody musta—"

"Put it in there," Mandie interrupted. Sliding off the bed, she stood up and looked at Celia. "You know who."

"Right," Celia agreed.

"Now, who dat be wantin' to put a mouse in yo' chifforobe?" Aunt Phoebe asked.

"Can't you even guess?" Mandie asked.

"You mean dat tall, black-headed, black-eyed gal wid a Yankee mama—whut's her name?"

"April Snow," Mandie answered. "You see, she told us when we left that we'd better enjoy our holidays because we might not enjoy coming back."

"But, Mandie, we don't know for sure that it was April," Celia reminded her.

"No, we don't. So, Aunt Phoebe, please don't tell anyone we thought it might be her," Mandie requested.

"I won't mention huh name, Missy 'Manda, but I will tell Miz Prudence dat a mouse got in yo' room," the Negro woman promised. "I'se gwine hafta put some rat poison out to git rid of it."

"Thanks, Aunt Phoebe," Mandie said with relief.

After helping the girls hang up the rest of their clothes, Aunt Phoebe hurried back into the hallway to finish her sweeping.

Mandie and Celia put their stockings and underthings in the drawers of the bureau and placed their bonnets in hat boxes on top of the chifforobe. Leaving personal belongings such as jewelry and letters in the trays of their trunks, they locked the lids.

Mandie stood up with the trunk key in her hand. "I think I'd feel safer about my trunk if I put this key on a ribbon around my neck," she said. "I can slip it under my dress. What do you think, Celia?"

"That's a good idea. I have some odd pieces of ribbon." Celia walked over to the bureau and pulled a handful of ribbons out of one of the drawers. "What color do you want?"

"Any color," Mandie said. "I think I have some extra ribbons, too."

"I have plenty here," Celia insisted. "I think you ought to take the blue one. It matches your eyes."

"But it won't show, so it doesn't matter what color it is," Mandie said, taking the blue ribbon.

"Well, you'll know what color it is anyway. I'll use the green one." Celia pulled out a bright green ribbon and carefully threaded it through the hole in her key as Mandie fixed hers. They tied the ends together, hung the ribbons around their necks, and dropped the keys out of sight inside their dresses.

"If somebody put that mouse in our chifforobe, it had to be April Snow," Mandie said, still nervously looking around on the floor.

"I think so, too, but we can't prove it," Celia agreed. "I just feel like I'm going to step on it any minute."

"Aunt Phoebe will get rid of it for us," Mandie assured her. "Let's sit down."

Sitting on the window seat, the two girls looked out at the bare limbs of the magnolia trees standing on the brown grass below.

"I'll be glad when Saturday comes," Mandie said. "Joe will be here then, and we can go back to the church."

"We can't unless we spend the weekend with your grandmother," Celia reminded her. "Miss Prudence would never let us go that far away from school."

"I thought you knew," Mandie said with a smile. "Grandmother promised to send Ben for us Friday after classes, and we won't have to come back here until Sunday afternoon."

"Oh, great!" Celia said excitedly. "We'll have all that time to work on the mystery."

The big bell in the backyard began ringing, beckoning the students to supper.

"Let's go," Mandie said, leading the way. The two girls hurried downstairs to wait in line outside the dining room door.

When Aunt Phoebe opened the French doors, the girls streamed into the dining room and took their assigned places, standing behind their chairs. No one was allowed to talk in the dining room, so they waited silently until all the girls were in. Then Miss Prudence Heathwood, the school's headmistress and sister of Miss Hope, entered from the other side of the room and took her place behind the chair at the head of the table.

As they stood there waiting, Mandie and Celia noticed that Etrulia had taken April Snow's place beside Mandie and April stood behind the chair directly across the table from them—where Etrulia ordinarily sat. They must have had permission to swap seats Mandie reasoned, because when Miss Prudence looked around the table, she did not mention the switch.

Miss Prudence picked up the little silver bell by her plate and shook it. All eyes turned in her direction.

"Young ladies, welcome back to all of you," Miss Prudence said. "I have an announcement to make. Our school is investing in those modern lights that work on electricity."

The students glanced at one another, not daring to say a word.

Miss Prudence continued. "A socket with a light bulb in it will be installed in each room. Hanging down from this socket will be a chain which you will pull to turn the light on and off. You have all seen this kind of light downtown at Edwards' Dry Goods Store, haven't you?"

"Yes, ma'am," the girls replied almost in unison.

"Good. Then you understand what I'm talking about," she said. "Now, there will be workmen coming in tomorrow, but y'all do not have permission to carry on conversations with these men. You will stay out of whatever room they are working on until they've finished. Do you understand?"

"Yes, Miss Prudence," the girls responded all around the table.

"After the lights are installed," the headmistress continued, "there will be more workmen coming to put in one of those large furnaces in the basement. This will be connected by metal ducts to what they call a radiator in each room. The house will be heated this way, and we will discontinue fires in the fireplaces except for emergencies and special occasions. You are not to talk to these workmen either. Are there any questions?"

"No, Miss Prudence," the girls said, again quickly exchanging glances.

Although the girls were curious about these modernization efforts, they dared not question Miss Prudence. The headmistress had a way of making a person look dumb. They'd find out about all this from someone else.

"Now, young ladies," Miss Prudence said, "we will return our thanks." After waiting for the girls to bow their heads, she spoke, "Our gracious Heavenly Father, we thank Thee for this food of which we are about to partake, and we ask Thy blessings on it and on all who are present. Amen. Young ladies, you may be seated now."

With the noise of scraping chairs, the girls sat down. The dining room held only half of the students. Mandie and Celia were in the first sitting.

Mandie kept an eye on April Snow throughout the entire meal, but the girl never once looked across the table. April completely ignored Mandie and Celia, quickly disappearing as soon as the girls were dismissed.

Mandie and Celia joined the other girls in the parlor after the meal.

Mandie looked around. "April Snow isn't in here," she said quietly to Celia.

"Maybe we should go back to our room," Celia suggested. "She might be up to something."

"You're right. Let's go."

They cautiously entered their room, fearing that the mouse might be there or that April might be lurking nearby. But the room was empty.

As Mandie looked around the floor for the mouse, she noticed white powder along the mopboard. "Aunt Phoebe must have put something on the floor to kill the mouse," she remarked.

"She said she was going to put out something," Celia agreed.

The girls sat down on the window seat and looked out into the early winter darkness. The wind blew hard against the windowpane, but the fire in their fireplace kept the room cozy and warm.

"I wonder how April got Miss Prudence's permission to swap seats at the table," Mandie mused. "You know she has never allowed that before."

"At least not while we've been going to school here," Celia added.

"April must have finagled that while we were gone home for Thanksgiving," Mandie decided. "I just know she must have been the one who put the mouse in our chifforobe."

"But how would she catch the mouse in the first place?" Celia wondered aloud.

"I sure wouldn't want to catch a mouse. Ugh!" Mandie shivered at the thought. She changed the subject. "What did you think of Miss Prudence's announcement at supper?"

"It'll be nice to have lights overhead, won't it?" Celia replied. "We have that kind at home, and it makes a big difference. We'll be able to see to read better at night."

"I suppose so," Mandie answered. "We don't have electricity or radiators, you know. My Uncle John has enough money to afford it. I don't know why he doesn't get all those things done. It would be less work for everybody. Even the church downtown here in Asheville has lights run by electricity, you know."

"But they don't have heat with radiators. Remember all those iron stoves sitting around the sanctuary?" Celia said.

"I know. Maybe Grandmother would donate enough money to put in the heat someday," Mandie speculated. "I suppose sooner or later everybody will have all these new lights and heat."

"Talking about the church, do you think we'll ever find

out who that man and woman in the church were?"

"Probably. If we just keep working on the mystery of the bells, I think we can solve the mystery of the strangers, too," Mandie replied, thoughtfully leaning her elbow against the window. "I'm still puzzled about that loud thumping noise and whatever made the belfry shake while we were up there. I believe everything that has happened is all connected."

"I think so, too," Celia agreed, watching her feet for any sign of the mouse.

There was a knock at the door and Aunt Phoebe came in and looked around. "Y'all ain't seen no sign of dat mouse no mo', has y'all?"

"No, Aunt Phoebe," Mandie replied. "Maybe the stuff you put around the mopboard got him."

"Stuff 'round de mopboard?" the Negro woman asked. "I ain't put nothin' 'round de mopboard. Where?"

"That white stuff down there." Celia pointed to some of it by the bureau.

"Lawsy mercy, Missies. I ain't put dat on de flo'," the old woman said, bending to look closely at the white powder.

"Then I wonder who did and what it is," Mandie said, stooping down beside her.

Aunt Phoebe stuck her finger in the white powder and smelled it. Straightening up, she looked on top of the bureau, picked up Mandie's powder jar and opened it. "Heah be whut dat is," she said. "Somebody done dumped all yo' bath powder on de flo'."

"Oh, for goodness' sakes!" Mandie exclaimed. "What is going to happen next?"

"I comes to tell y'all I be up heah fust thing after y'all goes to yo' schoolrooms in de mawnin'," Aunt Phoebe informed them. "I be gwine to put some liquid stuff dat you cain't see 'round de flo'. But it stink good, so I waits fo' y'all to leave yo' room. And jes' y'all 'member. Dis liquid stuff deadly poison."

"We'll be careful about dropping anything on the floor," Mandie promised.

"Dis stuff be dried up in no time after I puts it 'round," Aunt Phoebe told them. "Jes' leave dis white powder, and I'll clean it up in de mawnin'."

"Thank you, Aunt Phoebe," Mandie said. "April Snow probably did it, but we don't know for sure."

"I he'p you watch out fo' dat girl," the old woman said, shaking her head as she walked out the door. "She gwine hafta stop dis nonsense."

"Maybe we ought to talk to Miss Hope about the things that are going on," Celia suggested.

"What could we say?" Mandie asked. "We don't have any proof. Let's go find April and follow her around to see what she's doing."

"That's a good idea," Celia agreed.

The two girls left their room, walking slowly down the hallways, looking about for April Snow. She was nowhere to be seen. They returned to the parlor. There she was, sitting alone in a corner, reading the newspaper while the other students sat around talking.

Mandie and Celia looked at each other, then took a seat in two vacant chairs near Etrulia and Dorothy, a girl they didn't know very well.

Etrulia turned to them and said, "We've all been reading the newspaper. They say the whole town is angry about the bells in the church downtown. And now, because the bells are ringing thirteen times, they claim something bad is about to happen."

"That's just superstition," Mandie said. "The bells couldn't cause something bad to happen just because they're ringing wrong."

"I know that," Etrulia conceded, "but you know this town is full of superstitious people. They can really get everyone wound up about something like this."

"What else does the newspaper say?" Celia asked.

"Oh, there are several articles about it," Etrulia replied. "When April finishes reading it, y'all ought to look it over. Someone has even been writing on the back wall of the church."

Mandie and Celia looked at each other.

"When does this newspaper come out? What time of day?" Mandie asked.

Etrulia looked puzzled. "I suppose it comes out in the afternoon," she replied. "At least that's when the school gets it. You know it takes hours and hours to set up the presses and print it and then deliver it. I imagine they work on it all morning and then deliver it in the afternoon. That's what my father does. He owns the newspaper back home."

"You mean whatever news the paper has in it would have been collected early in the morning in order to be out in the afternoon?" Mandie questioned her.

"As far as I know, all the news has to be in by eight o'clock in the morning in order to be printed for the afternoon," Etrulia answered. "Why are you asking all this?"

"I was just curious about when the writing on the church wall was discovered," Mandie replied. "It must have been early this morning or last night, then."

"Yes," Etrulia agreed. "I sure hope they catch whoever is doing such disgraceful things."

Mandie nodded. "I do, too," she said.

Etrulia moved on across the room with some of the other girls while Mandie and Celia talked quietly.

"So we know the writing wasn't done while we were in the church," Mandie said hardly above a whisper.

"That's right," Celia agreed. "It would have had to be a lot earlier."

"Maybe someone did it in the dark when no one could

see them," Mandie suggested. "I'm just itching to solve this mystery."

"Well," Celia said with a sigh, "as soon as Friday comes, we can get started."

April laid the newspaper down and walked over to the piano as one of the girls began playing.

Mandie picked up the paper. The front page was full of news stories about the town's reactions to the bells ringing the wrong hour and the vandalism at the church. The only other news item on the front page was a story of a bank robbery in Charlotte the week before, which officials were still investigating.

*So many things are happening,* Mandie thought, *and they don't seem to be related at all.*

## Chapter 4 / Concern for Hilda

Aunt Phoebe used the rat poison in Mandie and Celia's room the next morning. As she promised, it soon dried up, and the odor went away. There was no sign of the mouse, alive or dead.

As the week dragged by, April Snow seemed to avoid Mandie and Celia, and they didn't go out of their way looking for her, either. They did, however, stay alert for any mischief she might do.

Finally, Friday came.

Mandie and Celia, with their bags nearby, sat waiting in the alcove near the center hallway of the school. They watched through the floor-length windows for Ben to come in Mrs. Taft's rig.

Mandie sprang from her chair. "I hear him coming!" she cried, grabbing her bag. "I know Ben's driving. He's just aflying."

As the rig came within sight, the girls hurried outside onto the veranda. They were so excited about leaving school for the weekend that they didn't even feel the cold north wind blowing around them. The sky was cloudy with a promise of rain or possibly snow.

Ben halted the rig in the curved driveway, and the girls ran down the steps. Joe Woodard was with him.

"Joe!" Mandie exclaimed. "I didn't think you'd be in town until tomorrow."

Joe, tall and lanky for his fourteen years, jumped down from the rig and held out Snowball, Mandie's white kitten. "Well, I could go home and take Snowball with me, and come back tomorrow," he teased.

Mandie snatched the kitten from him and cuddled it. "Now, Joe," she said, "you know I'm glad you could come today. We're just snowed under with mysteries."

Joe ran his long, thin fingers through his unruly brown hair. "Fixing to get into trouble again, are you?" he teased.

Ben put the girls' bags in the rig and everyone climbed aboard.

"No, we aren't," Mandie argued.

"Not if we can help it," Celia added.

Ben held the reins loosely in his hands and waited for a lull in the conversation. "Is y'all ready to proceed now?" he asked. "Miz Taft, she say hurry back. We better git a move on."

"Of course, Ben. Let's go," Joe said.

With a slap of the reins, the horses took off at a fast trot down the cobblestoned streets toward Grandmother Taft's house.

Joe listened as the girls related what had happened since they returned to school. "And I suppose y'all want me to help solve this problem of the bells ringing wrong," he said.

Ben drew the rig up in Mrs. Taft's driveway.

Mandie smiled sweetly. "Of course," she replied, jumping down from the vehicle.

"Yes," Celia agreed, following Mandie. "Three heads are better than two."

Joe's long strides caught up with the girls as Ella, the Negro maid, opened the front door.

"Miz Taft, she be in de parlor," Ella informed them.

"Ben, you take dem bags on upstairs. Miz Taft, she be in a hurry to see dese girls."

"Yes, ma'am, Miz Housekeeper," Ben replied sarcastically. He took the other bag from Joe and headed for the stairs.

Joe's father, Dr. Woodard, waited in the parlor with Mrs. Taft. After exchanging greetings, the young people sat down together on a nearby settee.

Mandie cuddled Snowball in her lap. "I'm glad y'all could come a day early, Dr. Woodard," she said.

The doctor cleared his throat. "Well, you see, your grandmother sent for me." He looked to Mrs. Taft to explain.

"Sent for you?" Mandie looked at her grandmother, puzzled.

"Now, don't get excited, Amanda," Mrs. Taft said. "But Hilda is sick. She—"

"Hilda? Sick?" Mandie interrupted. "Is it bad?"

"Amanda," Mrs. Taft reprimanded. "Please wait until I have finished talking before you get excited. Yes, Hilda is sick. She has pneumonia—"

"Pneumonia!" Mandie cried. "That's what took my father out of this world. Oh, is it bad, Dr. Woodard?" She dropped Snowball in Joe's lap and ran to stoop at Dr. Woodard's knee.

Dr. Woodard smoothed her blonde hair. "I'm afraid it could get bad," he said. He had been Jim Shaw's doctor back in the spring in Swain County.

Mandie jumped up. "Where is she?" she demanded. "Where is Hilda?"

"She's upstairs in her bedroom, dear," Dr. Woodard replied. "We've got a special nurse staying with her."

"I want to go see her," Mandie said, turning to leave the room.

"No, Amanda!" Mrs. Taft called sharply. "Hilda is not allowed to have any visitors. We don't want everyone else to catch this and come down sick, too."

With tears in her blue eyes, Mandie turned back and dropped onto the settee.

Joe reached for her hand and held it tight. "I know you're thinking about your father, Mandie," he said softly. "But don't. It won't help. It will only make it worse."

Snowball stepped over into his mistress's lap, curled up again, and began purring.

"Mrs. Taft, we were just here this past Tuesday, and Hilda was visiting with the Smiths. Did she get sick all of a sudden?" Celia asked.

"Yes, they brought her home that night, and she was running a high fever," Mrs. Taft replied. "When she didn't seem to get any better, I sent for Dr. Woodard, and he got here this afternoon."

"We've done all we can do right now," Dr. Woodard told Mandie. "We just have to pray that the Lord will heal her."

As a tear rolled down her cheek, Mandie lifted her head and began to pray softly. "Oh, dear God," she said, "please heal Hilda. She has been through so much, and now that things are getting better for her, please let her live to enjoy it."

The others joined in with their prayers. When they were finished, Mandie took Joe's handkerchief and dried her eyes.

"I remember how Hilda looked when we found her in the attic," Celia said. "She was so scared of us, and so starved-looking. Then she found out we were her friends, and she started getting better."

"The poor girl had never had any friends," Joe added. "Imagine her parents keeping her shut up in a room just because she wouldn't—or couldn't—talk."

"But she *can* talk," Mandie said firmly. "She is beginning to say a lot of words. She just never had a chance to learn because her parents thought she was demented."

"Well, she is not real bright, but she has more sense than people give her credit for," Dr. Woodard said. "And I can see that with the proper care and attention, like Mrs. Taft has been giving her, she could eventually lead an almost normal life."

"You'll keep watch over her, won't you, Dr. Woodard?" Mandie begged.

"I'll be here for the weekend. Then I have to go back to Swain County to see some sick folks there," the doctor replied. "But the nurse we have up there now knows what she's doing, and another nurse will relieve her at bedtime. Hilda won't be left alone."

"Thank you, Dr. Woodard," Mandie said. "Thanks to you and the Lord, she's going to pull through. I just know it."

After a short silence, Celia changed the subject. "Mrs. Taft, has anything else happened at the church since Mandie and I were there?" she asked, pushing back her long auburn hair.

"The church keeps having different people investigate, but they can't find anything wrong," Mrs. Taft replied.

"That's because there is nothing wrong with the clock or the bells," Mandie declared, straightening her shoulders. "It's just some person doing something that no one can catch them doing."

"But, Mandie, we were there when the bells rang thirteen times for twelve noon, remember? And there was no one there at all except us," Celia reminded her.

"They were just too quick for us, but we'll catch them sooner or later," Mandie predicted. "Just you wait and see."

"What about the man and the woman we saw in the church, Mrs. Taft?" Celia asked. "Did you find out anything about them?"

"No, dear," Mrs. Taft replied. "I've asked about them everywhere, but no one seems to have seen them enter or leave the church. And, according to the description y'all gave me of them, I don't believe they are people I know."

"Why didn't y'all follow them when they left the church?" Joe asked. "Or at least watch from the door when they went outside?"

"Because that was when the bells started ringing," Mandie explained, "and we had to go up to the belfry to see if anyone was up there."

"Hmm, I might as well ask," Joe said. "When do we visit the church to look for clues?"

Mandie and Celia both looked at Mrs. Taft.

"I suppose you young people could go some time in the morning after it warms up a little," she said.

"Thanks, Grandmother," Mandie said. She turned to Joe. "We'll go early enough so we'll be back in time for dinner, Joe," she added.

"Oh, good. I absolutely refuse to miss a meal, especially from your grandmother's table," Joe teased.

"I sure hope there's not any more shaking and thumping in that belfry," Celia remarked. "I don't know how we're ever going to figure out what that was. It must have been something awfully strong to shake the belfry that way."

"Either the shaking caused the thumping, or the thumping caused the shaking," Mandie figured. "It was all so fast and so close together, it must have been connected."

"That has me puzzled, Amanda," Mrs. Taft said. "That church is well built, and I can't imagine anything shaking any part of it unless it was an earthquake. But it seems no one else in town felt anything, so it couldn't have been an earthquake."

"Don't worry about it, Mrs. Taft. We'll figure it all out," Joe assured her.

Mandie gasped. "Oh, goodness!" she cried. "I just remembered something. The full moon is tomorrow, and that's when Uncle Ned promised to come to see me. He won't know I'm here and not at the school."

"Well, you could go to Aunt Phoebe's house tomorrow night and watch for him," Mrs. Taft said, "provided Joe and Celia go with you. Since Aunt Phoebe's house is right there in the backyard of the school, it ought to be safe enough, don't you think, Dr. Woodard?"

"I'm sure they'll be safe with Aunt Phoebe and Uncle Cal," the doctor answered. "They're good people."

"But Grandmother, Uncle Ned doesn't come to visit until after curfew at ten o'clock so that no one at the school will see him," Mandie explained. "He always waits under the huge magnolia tree right down below our bedroom window."

Uncle Ned was an old Cherokee friend of Mandie's father. When Jim Shaw had died, Uncle Ned had promised him he would watch over Mandie. And he kept his word. He regularly visited her and knew everything that was going on where she was concerned.

"If it's going to be late, I'll send Ben with y'all. He'll have to take y'all over there anyway. I'll tell him to wait for y'all," Mrs. Taft said.

"Grandmother, could we leave here in time to go by the church and check it out again tomorrow night before we go to Aunt Phoebe's?" Mandie begged. "Please?"

"Why, Amanda, I thought you were all going to the church tomorrow morning," Mrs. Taft replied.

"We are, but we should go to the church as many times as possible because you never know when we might find something to solve the mystery," Mandie insisted.

"Let's have one thing understood here and now, Amanda," Mrs. Taft said firmly. "You are not to go to the church without Ben or another adult with you at any time.

And that applies to you, Celia. Don't you agree, Dr. Woodard?"

"Yes, ma'am," the doctor said. "There's no telling who or what you might run into at the church, and I certainly don't want Joe going there without an adult. In fact, I forbid it. Remember that, Joe."

"Yes, sir," Joe answered quickly. "I'd like to have an adult along anyway to back me up in case of trouble. These two girls wouldn't be much help if something unexpected happened."

Mandie glared at Joe. "I can remember a few times when *you* needed *our* help, Joe Woodard," she said. "Celia and I are both twelve years old, and you are only two years older."

Snowball jumped down to the floor and scampered out of the room. "I know. I know," Joe agreed. "Time about is fair enough."

"Remember the time the Catawbas kidnapped you, and—" Mandie began.

"I said, all right," Joe interrupted.

"Well, then," Mandie said, and turning to her grandmother asked, "Is it all right then for us to go to the church before we go to Aunt Phoebe's house since Ben will be with us?"

"Amanda, you know it will be dark then," Mrs. Taft reminded her. "It gets dark early now."

"But the church has those electric lights in it," Mandie persisted.

"If we can find the strings in the dark to pull them on," Celia said.

"If we light up the church, everyone in town will know it," Joe objected. "And if there's anyone messing around there, they'll run away fast."

Mandie thought for a moment. "Could we take a lantern with us, Grandmother?" she asked.

"I suppose so," Mrs. Taft agreed reluctantly. "Just

don't stay out too late. Keep your visit with Uncle Ned short. And be sure you stay within sight of Ben at all times."

"Thanks, Grandmother," Mandie said. "We will. I promise."

Little did Mandie know how impossible that promise would be to keep.

## Chapter 5 / Trapped!

"You are not taking that white cat, are you?" Joe asked Mandie as the three young people put on their coats the next morning.

Mandie looked down at Snowball, who was sitting on the arm of the hall tree watching. "No, I guess not," she said. "He might get away from me and—"

"And get lost." Joe finished her sentence. "And then we'd have to go looking for him."

"All right," Mandie agreed. She turned to Celia. "Are you ready?"

"All ready," Celia replied, tying her bonnet under her chin.

Mandie stooped to look into the eyes of her kitten. "Now, Snowball, you stay here in the house," she cautioned. "Don't you dare go outside."

Snowball meowed in response and sat watching as the three young people opened the front door and went outside.

They all climbed aboard the waiting rig, Ben shook the reins, and they were off.

"Tell me again about that shaking in the belfry," Joe said.

"I think it was the floor up there," Mandie replied.

"Or was it the whole belfry trembling?" Celia asked.

"It could have been, but it seems like I felt my feet shaking," Mandie said.

Celia laughed. "I was shaking all over. That's for sure."

"You two are a big help," Joe said, exasperated. "How can I find out what caused something when I don't even know what it was?"

"We certainly don't know what it was," Mandie said.

"But if you could remember exactly *what* was shaking, it might help me figure out what was going on," Joe urged.

Ben pulled the rig up sharply in front of the church, and Mandie jumped down. "Anyway, here we are," she announced. "You can go up there yourself and look around."

"Yo' grandma, she say fo' me to wait right heah fo' y'all," Ben told Mandie.

"Please do, Ben," Mandie said. "If you get cold, come inside the church."

"It nice and warm under dis heah lap robe," Ben said. "I jes' wait heah."

The young people hurried inside the church and looked around the sanctuary. There was no one in sight.

Mandie led the way. "The door and steps to the gallery are right over here," she told Joe, taking off her coat. "Let's leave our coats down here. It's not that cold now, and they'll just get in the way."

After taking off their coats and leaving them on a back pew, Joe and Celia followed her up the stairs and across the balcony.

"Then this door here leads to the belfry," Mandie said, opening the door and showing Joe the bells overhead.

"And this must be the rope ladder." Joe grasped it and quickly skimmed upward.

As he swung off at the top, Mandie started climbing. Celia stayed where she was.

"Aren't you coming, Celia?" Mandie called down to her.

"I think I'll just stay down here and watch out for y'all," she replied nervously.

Mandie and Joe explored the belfry. They examined the floor and walls as well as the support the bells were anchored to. There was nothing loose.

"I know something was shaking when we were up here," Mandie declared. "I didn't imagine it."

"As far as I can tell, though, there is not even a loose board up here," Joe told her. "Could it have been the vibration of the bells ringing?"

"No, the bells weren't ringing when this happened," Mandie explained. "And don't forget, there was also a thumping noise, like something had fallen."

Joe inspected the wires to the bells. "How far away did the noise sound?" he asked.

"I suppose it could have come from downstairs in the sanctuary," Mandie reasoned. "But it sounded all muffled—a thick kind of noise. It wasn't a sharp sound."

"I think we should go back down and examine the whole church as we go," Joe suggested. "Maybe we can find something that has fallen."

"We thought the shaking and the noise must have been connected because everything happened so close together," Mandie explained, heading for the ladder. "I'm coming down, Celia," she called to her friend below. "Stay out of the way."

"All right," Celia answered. "Just don't come down too fast. You might fall."

Mandie quickly descended the rope ladder and jumped off the last rung. Joe followed.

"Did you find out anything up there?" Celia asked. She seemed relieved that she didn't have to climb the swinging ladder.

"No," Mandie replied, "but we're going to search the whole church now."

Joe looked around the balcony. "Let's begin here,"

he said. "Go up and down each row of benches and look for anything that might be loose or anything that might have fallen."

The three young people quickly covered the gallery and found nothing of interest.

"I guess we can go down to the sanctuary, then," Joe said, leading the way downstairs.

"Why don't we leave the sanctuary to the last and work our way through the basement first," Mandie suggested. "Then we can come back through here on the way out."

"That's a good idea," Joe agreed. "Do y'all know how to get into the basement?"

"Sure," Celia answered. "We have our Sunday school classes in the basement."

"Through this doorway here by the choir loft," Mandie said, pointing.

She opened a door to a hallway with Sunday school rooms opening off the sides and a stairway at the far end. The windows in the rooms shed a little light into the hallway.

Joe looked around. "This sure is a big church," he remarked. "They have classrooms back here and more in the basement?"

Mandie laughed. "There are a lot of good people in Asheville, so it takes a huge church to hold them," she said. "Besides, most of the people who belong to this church have a lot of money."

Joe headed down the stairs and the girls followed. At the bottom, they came to a door that opened into a hallway much darker than the one above. Since the basement was half sunk into the ground, the rooms off the hallway only had small windows near the ceiling.

"It's so dark down here I think we should all stay together," Celia suggested. There was a little quiver in her voice. "Someone could be hiding in this basement."

"You're right, Celia," Joe agreed. "Let's start on this side over here."

Starting with the first classroom on the right, they searched each room up and down the hallway.

"The only things in these rooms are a few chairs and a table," Joe observed, "so there isn't really any place for anyone to hide."

"That thumping noise could have been caused by almost anything, though," Mandie said.

They all shook a few of the chairs and tables along the way to see if any of them were wobbly. In one room they found an easel, but it seemed to be standing on strong legs. On the easel stood a piece of cardboard with a map roughly drawn on it in various colors. Nearby were several small cans of water-color paint.

"What's down there at the end of the hall?" Joe asked, heading in that direction.

"It's the room where all the classes gather for a song every Sunday before we go upstairs for the preacher's sermon," Mandie replied.

Joe surveyed the room. In the front there was a piano with a swivel stool on claw feet. Numerous chairs filled the rest of the room. "I think we've cleared the basement," he said. "Let's see what we can find in the classrooms upstairs."

The girls followed Joe back upstairs, searching each room that opened off the hallway. At the far end they came to the pastor's study.

Joe tried the door, but it wouldn't open. He looked puzzled. "I wonder why the preacher locked his office," he said.

"He farms way out in the country," Mandie explained, "so he probably does all his pastor work in his house. As far as I know, he comes to the church only when there's a service."

"Well, he still didn't have to lock the door," Joe said in exasperation.

"Joe, this isn't Swain County where everyone leaves their doors open and unlocked," Mandie reminded him. "This is a big city. There are all kinds of people in this town. The church doors are unlocked all day. Anyone could come in."

"Yes, even strangers, like the man and woman we saw here the other day," Celia added.

"Oh, well," Joe said with a sigh, "if we can't get inside that locked room, then neither can anyone else."

"Unless they have a key," Mandie said. "And I imagine the only people who have keys are the pastor, and the sexton, and maybe some of the deacons."

"All right, let's go," Joe said.

Inside the sanctuary they wandered toward the back. Then suddenly all three of them noticed something down at the altar.

"There's a flag or something there," Celia said, pointing.

"Or a banner." Mandie hurried forward.

Joe said nothing but took quick strides down the center aisle.

There, tied around the altar, was something that looked like a large piece of a white bed sheet with big red letters painted on it—just one word—*HELP!* The three young people stood there for several seconds just staring at it.

Mandie walked closer to inspect the cloth. "I'd say this is a piece of one of the choir robes," she said, feeling the material.

Joe bent to look at the lettering. "And the red paint came from the water colors we saw by the easel in one of the rooms downstairs," he said.

"Where do they keep the choir robes?" Celia asked. "Don't the choir members take their robes home with them?"

Mandie thought for a moment. "I imagine they do

most of the time, but someone could have left one in the church," she said. "Or maybe it was an extra one that no one was using."

"Should we take this thing down?" Joe asked.

"First, let's look for the rest of the robe," Mandie suggested. "It looks like that's only half of it."

"But, Mandie, we've been all over the church," Celia protested.

"I know we've been everywhere, but I don't believe this was here when we came in," Mandie argued. "We would have noticed it."

"You mean someone is here in the church?" Celia's voice was barely a whisper.

Joe puzzled over the matter. "Why would anyone put the word *help* on half a choir robe and hang it on the altar?"

"If we could find whoever did it, then we'd know," Mandie replied. "So I think we ought to look for that person."

"Let's stay together," Celia warned, "now that we know someone else is in the church."

The three young people again went through the entire church, finding nothing and no one.

As they returned to the sanctuary Joe spoke up. "I suppose we might as well remove that thing from the altar," he said.

But as they started down the aisle, Mandie caught her breath. "Look!" She rushed forward. "It's gone!"

Joe and Celia ran after her. Sure enough, the piece of cloth was gone. They looked all around, but there was no sign of it anywhere. Then the bells started ringing.

The young people stood still to silently count the rings. It was twelve noon, but how many times would the bells toll?

"Eleven, twelve," Mandie finished her count aloud. "It was right this time."

"We'd better go," Joe said. "Your grandmother will have dinner ready by now."

"I feel like having a good meal, myself," Mandie replied.

"Me, too," Celia agreed.

When the three returned to the rig, Ben was fast asleep under the lap robe, and they had to wake him.

The Negro driver sat up and yawned. "Y'all gone so long I jes' had to take me a nap," he said.

"Well, it's time to eat, Ben," Joe told him as the three piled into the rig.

When they got back to the house, they related their morning's adventures to Mrs. Taft and Dr. Woodard. No one had any explanations.

The conversation turned to other matters, and Dr. Woodard assured the young people that Hilda was resting comfortably—no worse, but no better than when they had left that morning.

Caught up in the excitement of their adventure, the young people counted the hours until they could return to the church that night.

When the time finally came to leave, Mrs. Taft gave the Negro driver strict instructions. "Now, Ben, you be sure you keep close tabs on these young people to see that no one harms them."

"Yessum, I will," Ben promised.

The young people didn't tell Mrs. Taft that Ben always stayed outside the church and that he even went to sleep.

It was dark when they reached the church, but the full moon shone brightly, and Joe had brought a lantern and plenty of matches to look around inside.

Ben stayed outside in the rig while the three noiselessly entered the church. Inside the vestibule, they looked around the sanctuary, which was dimly illuminated by the moonlight shining through the stained glass windows.

Joe took charge. "Let's not light the lantern until we have to," he suggested, heading for the stairs to the gallery.

"It'll be pitch dark on the stairways and in the basement," Celia said.

"And remember, we don't have very long if we're going to get to Aunt Phoebe's house in time to see Uncle Ned," Mandie reminded him.

"Y'all come on with me upstairs," Joe said, opening the door to the gallery. "I'll run up in the belfry and check it out."

Once upstairs, the three crossed the gallery in the dim light.

Joe opened the door to the belfry. "Wait right here," he told the girls, handing Mandie the lantern.

After disappearing up the rope ladder for a few minutes, he called softly to them, telling them he was coming back down. Landing with a jump, he said, "There's nothing going on up there. Let's look through the classrooms." He took the lantern from Mandie and headed down the stairs.

They hurriedly inspected the classrooms behind the altar, then turned to go down to the basement.

Mandie stopped at the head of the stairs. "It's too dark to see, Joe," she said. "We're going to have to light the lantern."

"I guess we'd better," Joe agreed. "We don't want to fall." Taking a match from his pocket and striking it on the sole of his shoe, he lit the lantern.

The light seemed bright after their eyes had become accustomed to the darkness of the church. Joe descended the stairs first, holding the lantern high so the girls could see. At the bottom of the stairs, the hallway was even darker. Thick shrubbery outside the small, high windows in the classrooms blocked the moonlight, and the lantern light threw weird shadows.

"It's spooky down here," Celia said.

Neither Joe nor Mandie responded, but the young people stayed close together as they crept from room to room, searching for clues. They ended up at the far end of the hallway.

"Nothing," Joe said with a sigh.

Just then there was a loud banging noise overhead. The three young people froze.

Celia grabbed Mandie's hand. "W-what was th-that?" she stuttered.

"Let's go find out," Joe whispered. Leading the way back down the hallway, he pushed on the door to the stairs. It wouldn't budge. "I'm afraid someone has locked this door," he said softly.

"Oh, goodness!" Celia cried. "What are we going to do?"

Mandie tried the door, too. It was definitely locked.

"Now we *know* someone is in the church," Joe said, pushing hard against the door again. "And that someone has locked us in here."

Mandie's heart pounded. "What are we going to do, Joe?" she asked. "We've got to get out of here and go to Aunt Phoebe's house."

Just as Joe was about to say something, the lantern dimmed and went out. Everyone gasped.

"Don't worry," Joe said. "I have some more matches." He struck a match to relight the lantern and touched the match to the wick. The lantern sputtered and went out. He tried another match. When it did the same thing, he lit another match to examine the lantern by its light. "Oh, no!" he exclaimed. "The lantern is out of oil! I'm sorry. It's my fault. I just grabbed a lantern out of your grandmother's pantry, Mandie, and I didn't bother to see how much oil there was in it."

"Oh, Joe, we really are in trouble!" Mandie cried.

"We could try the windows," Joe suggested, turning back to a classroom.

"They have bars on the outside," Mandie explained. "And they're awfully small, anyway."

Again the banging noises began overhead. The young people huddled together in the darkness. Mandie's heart pounded so loudly that she was sure the others could hear it. Her legs buckled beneath her. All three of them plopped down on the floor by the locked door.

Then there was complete silence upstairs.

"We've got to get out of here!" Mandie cried. "There may be someone dangerous up there."

"It must be someone who has some keys," Joe said. "Otherwise, how could they lock that door?"

"These locks have a thumb latch," Mandie said nervously, "and the thumb latch on that door happens to be on the other side, so all they had to do was flip the latch to lock us in here."

Celia squeezed Mandie's hand tightly. "Oh, Mandie, whatever are we going to do?"

"Let's say our verse that always helps when we get in trouble," Mandie said.

The three young people joined hands and repeated the Bible verse that always gave them strength. "What time I am afraid," they recited, "I will put my faith in Thee."

Mandie took a deep breath and rose to her feet. "Now I won't be afraid because I know God will help us get out of this predicament somehow," she said. "He always does."

"I wish I knew what was going on upstairs," Joe said.

"Me, too," Celia agreed. "Whoever is up there could be a dangerous character."

The three walked about, softly discussing possibilities. Mrs. Taft would be worried when they didn't return, and Uncle Ned would be waiting under the magnolia tree in the cold for nothing.

Somehow they had to get out!

## Chapter 6 / No Way to Escape?

"I wish I hadn't suggested we leave our coats in the sanctuary," Mandie said, briskly rubbing her arms to warm herself. "Too bad there's nothing down here to build a fire in that big stove in the hallway."

"I'm cold, too," Celia complained, "and it's so spooky down here. What are we going to do?"

"We can't stay here all night," Joe said. "We've got to get out somehow."

Celia shivered as she paced back and forth on the cold concrete floor. "I wonder why Ben hasn't come looking for us."

"He probably fell asleep in the rig again," Mandie answered.

"Well, we've got to do something," Joe announced. "Let's try the windows. We might find some loose bars on one of them or something."

Celia looked up at the high windows. "I don't think we can reach them," she said.

"You're right, Celia," Mandie agreed. "I don't believe Joe can reach that high, either."

"I can always get taller," Joe said with a grin. He carried a chair over to the window and stood on it. "Like this," he added.

"You can just barely reach the window, Joe," Mandie

71

argued. "Celia and I would never be able to."

"Never mind. I'll check the windows myself," Joe answered.

The windows, which were locked by spring hooks, consisted of only one small pane, and they pulled out and down from the top like a door opening sideways.

Joe pulled the first one open and reached through to the bars outside. "No luck," he said. Shaking his head, he stepped down and moved the chair below the next window.

"I wish we could find something to knock the bars loose," Mandie said, looking around in the darkness.

"There's nothing here we can use," Joe reminded her as he opened the second window. "Remember, we checked the whole place."

Celia watched Joe trying to loosen the bars. "It'd probably be easier to break the door down than to knock out any of those iron bars," she commented.

"Let's try it, Celia," Mandie said. "We can work on the door while Joe works on the windows." The girls hurried out into the hallway.

"Hey, don't go hurting yourselves now," Joe cautioned. "That's an awfully strong door."

"We'll just see what we can do," Mandie called back to him. She felt her way through the darkness to the door at the end of the hallway. Celia clutched Mandie's shoulder and followed.

When they got to the door, Mandie ran her hands around the doorknob. "Oh, shucks!" she exclaimed. "The lock is on the other side, and the door opens into the hall this way. That means we have to pull on it instead of pushing."

Celia laid her hands on top of Mandie's on the doorknob. "Maybe it'll work," she said.

The girls tried to pull together on the door, but four hands wouldn't fit. Celia let go.

Mandie grasped the doorknob tightly. "I'll have to pull by myself," she said. She pulled as hard as she could, but the door didn't even rattle. The lock held fast. As Mandie shook her aching hands in the air, Celia stepped up for a try. Nothing happened.

"Maybe Joe could pull harder on it," Mandie said. "Come on, I'm going back there to see where he is."

The girls felt their way back down the dark hallway until they came to the end room where Joe was examining a window.

"Nothing yet," Joe said to them, running his hands over the bars outside. "As far as I can tell, all these bars are bolted into the brick and cement."

"And there's no way to get one loose," Mandie added. "Celia and I couldn't budge the door, either."

"What are we going to do?" Celia fretted.

"Now, Celia, don't forget. We're going to trust in God," Mandie reminded her friend. "Remember our verse?"

"I know," Celia whispered. "I just wish we could hurry up and get out of this place."

"Joe, why don't you stop working on those windows for a minute and see if you can do anything with that door?" Mandie suggested.

Joe stepped down, preparing to go on to the next window. "I only have these two left," he said, motioning to the ones on the end. "I've examined all the windows in the other rooms. I'll see what I can do with the door as soon as I'm finished here." Stepping up onto the chair, he inspected the bars on the window above him. "Just like the rest—solid," he said, stepping down and moving to the last window.

The girls watched silently as he climbed up, opened the window, and reached out to touch the iron bars.

He turned and grinned at them. "One corner is loose," he said excitedly. "If I can manage to get another corner free, we might be able to squeeze out."

Grabbing the bars with both hands, he shook them with all his strength. The loose corner wiggled a little, but the rest of the bars stayed firmly in place.

Finally Joe gave up. "Looks like we're in here to stay unless I can get the door open," he said. Closing the window, he stepped down from the chair.

"Maybe Ben will wake up and come looking for us," Mandie said hopefully.

"I don't imagine Ben will come inside the church when there aren't any lights on up there," Joe argued. "Let me try the door."

The three felt their way through the dark hallway to the door again. Joe took hold of the doorknob with both hands and pulled with all his might. Nothing happened. He released it, took a deep breath, braced his long legs, and yanked hard. Suddenly, he fell backward, knocking the girls behind him onto the floor.

"Land sakes!" Mandie cried, getting up from the hard floor. "What happened?"

"The blasted doorknob came off," Joe said, holding the knob in his hand. He stood up. "Maybe I can put it back on."

He felt around on the door for the place where the doorknob belonged. "The spindle that holds the knobs is gone!" he exclaimed. "So the other side of the knob is gone, too."

"How are we ever going to get out of here?" Celia asked.

"This is the back of the church, and Ben is parked on the road in front, but do you suppose if we yelled loud enough he might hear us?" Mandie asked.

"We could try," Joe said.

"If we could all get up there and open a window and yell, it might work." Celia sounded hopeful.

"The room where you found the loose bar has a big table in it, remember?" Mandie reminded Joe. "We could pull it over to the window and then put chairs on top of it. Celia and I ought to be able to stand on the chairs and reach the window."

"You might be able to if the chairs are steady enough," Joe said.

The three returned to the room where the table was. They pushed the table under the window with the loose iron bar, and set two chairs on top of it.

"Are y'all sure you won't fall?" Joe asked. "You could get hurt pretty bad, you know, on this concrete floor."

"At this point we just have to take chances," Mandie said. "But we'll be careful." She raised her long skirt and jumped up onto the table. Then swinging her legs around, she scrambled to her feet. Joe held the chair while she stepped up onto the seat. She looked up. Her head almost touched the ceiling in front of the window. "Come on up, Celia."

Celia copied Mandie's antics to get up on the other chair. Joe stood between the girls to support them and opened the window.

"Well, now that we're up here, what do we yell?" Joe asked.

"Let's just call Ben," Mandie said. Raising her voice, she started yelling. "Ben! Ben! Come to the back of the church!"

Celia and Joe joined in, and the three together hollered loud enough to wake the whole neighborhood.

Joe stopped to catch his breath. "He must be able to hear all the noise we're making," he said.

"Maybe he left," Celia suggested.

"No, Grandmother gave him strict orders not to leave us," Mandie said.

"Well, he's either gone off somewhere or he's deaf," Joe decided.

All three stood quietly for a minute as they tried to

look out through the thick shrubbery in front of the window.

Suddenly Mandie touched Joe's arm. "Did you see something move out there?" she whispered.

"I did!" Celia said quietly.

"Where?" Joe whispered back.

"There!" Mandie pointed through the shrubbery off to the left. "Do you suppose it's Ben?"

"I saw something move," Joe whispered.

Then the bushes quit shaking.

*It must be Ben*, Mandie thought. *Besides, if it were someone bad, he couldn't get in any more than we can get out*, she reasoned. She raised her voice again. "Ben! Ben!" she shouted. "We're in here!"

There was a quick movement in the shrubbery outside, then a familiar voice answered, "Papoose! Where Papoose?"

"Uncle Ned!" Mandie exclaimed as tears came to her eyes. "We're down here in the basement, Uncle Ned!"

Joe and Celia breathed sighs of relief along with Mandie as the old Indian moved between the bushes to the window and looked in through the iron bars.

"Papoose, Doctor Son, Papoose See," Uncle Ned called to them. (He called Celia *Papoose See* because he couldn't pronounce her name.) "How you get in there?" he demanded.

"Somebody locked the door, and we can't get out," Mandie explained. "Oh, Uncle Ned, you're the answer to our prayers."

"Please get us out, Uncle Ned!" Celia cried.

"Do you know where Ben is?" Joe queried.

"How did you know we were here?" Mandie asked.

"One time for each question," Uncle Ned replied. "First, must get out. Ben sleep. I get Ben." The old Indian turned to go.

"Wait, Uncle Ned," Mandie called to him. "The front

door is supposed to be unlocked. We came in that way. But somebody else has been in the church. Whoever it is locked the door at the bottom of the stairs."

"I go see," Uncle Ned nodded and hurried off.

"Oh, what a relief!" Celia climbed down from the chair and sat on the table.

Mandie and Joe sat down beside her.

"I guess Ben was asleep," Joe said in exasperation. "A lot of good it did to bring him with us!"

"Let's don't make trouble for him," Mandie suggested.

"We have to tell your grandmother the truth, Mandie," Joe said.

"But we don't have to go into detail," Mandie replied. "If she knows Ben went to sleep outside and we got locked in here alone, she might not let him go with us anywhere anymore, and then we might not be able to solve the mystery."

"If he goes with us anywhere else, he should stay right along with us and not take a nap outside," Joe said.

"You're right," Mandie agreed. "Next time we'll insist on that."

In a few minutes Uncle Ned reappeared at the basement window with Ben beside him. The girls quickly took their places on the chairs with Joe steadying them.

"Door locked," Uncle Ned announced. "Must think. Other way out?"

"Lawsy mercy, Missies, how y'all git in dat place all locked up like dat?" Ben called to them.

"We don't know, Ben," Mandie told him. "Someone locked the door to the basement while we were down here."

Joe reached out to touch the iron bars on the window. "These bars are loose in this one corner," he said, pointing. "I tried to get it loose enough for us to crawl out, but I didn't have any tools."

Uncle Ned examined the bars.

Ben watched as the old Indian shook the bars and thought for a minute. "I think I got a claw hammer in de rig," Ben said. "I go see."

"Please be sure you come right back, Ben," Mandie called after him.

"Yessum, Missy. I be back in a minute," the Negro replied.

Uncle Ned looked up from his examination of the bars. "Bars stuck good in cement. Hammer break cement. Much damage."

"I think my grandmother would pay for any damage we do, Uncle Ned—I hope," Mandie answered.

Ben returned with a large claw hammer. Everyone watched as the strong old Indian banged on the iron bars. The young people shielded their eyes as bits of cement flew through the air.

Uncle Ned shook the bars and hammered again. Then he turned to Ben. "You pull. I pull," he said.

Ben understood and braced himself to yank on the bars at the same time the old Indian did.

"Away!" Uncle Ned told the young people. "Bar come loose and cement hit papooses."

The three scrambled down and crouched on the table beneath the window, waiting.

"Pull!" Uncle Ned shouted.

There was a sudden, loud, cracking noise.

"One end loose," Uncle Ned announced.

The young people stood up to look.

"Must break other end," the old Indian fussed. He picked up the hammer from the ground. "Away!" he told the young people again.

Again they sat down, waiting and listening as Uncle Ned pounded and the wall vibrated with the hard blows. Cement flew everywhere. Mandie and Celia bent their heads to keep it from getting into their eyes. Joe moved away from the window to watch, and the girls followed.

Uncle Ned dropped the hammer. "Now!" he called to Ben.

Together the two men pulled and grunted. The bars wouldn't give. Uncle Ned picked up the hammer again and gave the bars a few more hard blows. Ben helped him pull again. Suddenly the bars gave way, and the two men fell backward into the shrubbery.

Mandie jumped back up on the chair to look out the now unbarred window. "Oh, thank you, Uncle Ned!" she cried.

The old Indian stood up and came over to the window. "Small to crawl through," he said, measuring the opening with his old wrinkled hands.

"I think it might be large enough," Joe said. "I can help the girls from in here if you can help them out up there."

"I help," Uncle Ned agreed.

The three young people happily chattered about who would be the first one out; then Mandie stopped suddenly. "I just remembered something!" she exclaimed. "Our coats—they're upstairs!"

"That's right!" Celia said.

"Well, I don't know how we're going to get up there with the basement door still locked," Joe told them. "And Uncle Ned said the front door was locked, too."

"We come in," Uncle Ned offered. "We open door down there."

"But Uncle Ned," Mandie said, "the doorknob is gone on both sides, and even the spindle dropped off."

"Me see." Uncle Ned turned to Ben. "We go down there. Me go first."

"Don't get stuck, Uncle Ned," Mandie called from below.

Taking his sling of arrows and his bow from his shoulder, he pushed them through the window. "Take," he told Joe.

Joe took them and moved out of the way.

Uncle Ned squatted down and stuck his long legs through the open window. As he slid in, his broad shoulders just barely made it through the opening. Ben, whose frame was even bigger than Uncle Ned's had a harder time, but when he finally landed on the table, both men sighed with relief and looked around.

"No light?" the Indian asked.

"No, Uncle Ned," Mandie replied. "Our lantern is out of oil."

Celia touched Mandie's arm. "Aren't there any of those new electric lights down here like there are upstairs?" she asked.

"I don't know," Mandie said, looking around. "If there are, there would be a string hanging from a fixture on the ceiling."

The group searched each room for any indication of electric lights, but they found none.

"Now, why would they have electric lights upstairs and none down here?" Joe wondered.

"They haven't had the lights upstairs very long," Celia replied. "They put them in since we came to school here in Asheville, and I seem to remember something about having to raise more money to wire the basement."

Mandie sighed in disappointment. "You're right, Celia," she said. "I remember now, too."

"What do you use for light when you're in the basement at night, then?" Joe asked.

"I don't think it's ever used at night," Mandie answered. "There are so many rooms upstairs that they don't really need it."

Uncle Ned spoke up. "Where door?" he asked, putting his sling of arrows over his shoulder again.

When they showed the door to him and Ben, Uncle

Ned felt around in the darkness. "Here knob hole," he said. "Notches inside."

"You see, there's no way to open it," Celia said.

"Never say no way anything," Uncle Ned replied. "Always way." He took one of his arrows from his sling, felt for the hole, and carefully inserted the tip of the arrow into it.

The young people and Ben hovered around, trying to see in the darkness. Uncle Ned slowly twisted the arrow, and they heard the click of the latch withdrawing in the lock. Carefully pulling on the door by the arrow in the lock, the old Indian gradually eased the door open.

Everyone gasped.

"But that door was locked!" Mandie exclaimed. "We couldn't turn the lock, remember?"

"It certainly was," Joe agreed. "And all Uncle Ned did was turn the latch and it opened. Someone has been playing tricks on us."

"You mean somebody locked it and then later unlocked the thumb latch on the other side?" Celia asked in disbelief.

"I guess so," Joe replied.

"Get coats," Uncle Ned urged. "Ben lock window."

Ben hurriedly latched the window as the young people started up the stairs.

Joe's foot kicked something, and he bent to pick it up. "Here's the other doorknob," he said, holding it out to Uncle Ned.

"Leave here. Must hurry," Uncle Ned urged.

When they all got upstairs, they found their coats just where they had left them in the last pew at the back of the sanctuary.

Celia hurriedly slipped into hers. "Thank goodness no one took our coats while we were trapped down there!" she exclaimed. "Oh, this feels nice and warm."

"Wait a minute," Mandie cried as Joe helped her into

her coat. "If the front door is locked, how are we going to get out of here?"

They all stopped and looked at each other, realizing Mandie was right.

Joe ran to try the front door. "It's locked, all right," he said, shaking his head.

"Is door in back?" Uncle Ned asked.

"You mean a back door?" Mandie replied. "I don't know. I don't think I've ever noticed. Let's go see."

They hurried to the back.

"I know where it is," Celia suddenly remembered. "It's in the back of the pastor's study. I remember seeing it once when the door to the study was open."

"And the pastor keeps his study locked," Joe reminded them. "Why would the back door be in the pastor's study?"

"His study was probably made out of the end of the hall. See?" Mandie pointed to the room down the hall. "And the door was probably already there."

"Oh, give me a country church anytime. These city churches are made too complicated," Joe moaned.

"Must go down, out window," Uncle Ned decided.

"Now, how's we gwine do dat?" Ben asked. "I almost didn't fit through dat window a-comin' in."

Mandie smiled. "Ben, if you fit coming in, you'll fit going out," she teased.

Uncle Ned led the way back down to the basement room where he and Ben had come in. "I go first," he said. "Then Ben. Be up there, help papooses get out. Doctor son last. Help papooses up. Take coats off and push through window."

They understood his plan. The old Indian gave Joe his bow and arrows and quickly scooted through the window. Joe handed the Indian's things back to him; then Ben started through. It took some squirming and twisting, but he made it all right. The young people removed their coats and pushed them through the window to the men above.

"Mandie, you go first," Joe suggested. "Then you can help Celia get out."

"All right," Mandie agreed, climbing onto the chair to reach the windowsill.

"When I get hold of your feet and push, you grab Uncle Ned's hands up there," Joe instructed.

Mandie did as she was told and soon found her feet firmly planted on the ground outside the window. She breathed a great sigh of relief.

Celia climbed through with no problem and then Joe followed, handing Uncle Ned the worthless empty lantern. He reached back inside to slam the window shut, hoping the latch would catch. It did.

Hastily putting on their coats in the bright moonlight, the young people ran out to the rig with Uncle Ned and Ben.

Mandie looked up into the old Indian's face. "How did you know we were here, Uncle Ned?" she asked.

"I go to school. Aunt Phoebe see, tell me Papoose at Grandmother house. I tell her I go to Grandmother. Aunt Phoebe not wait for Papoose now," the Indian explained. "On way to Grandmother, I see rig in front of church. Ben sleep. I know about bells. I know Papoose near."

"Then you heard us hollering our heads off," Mandie said with a nervous laugh.

Uncle Ned reached out and took her small hand in his old wrinkled one. "Papoose, what been doing?" he asked.

Mandie and the others related the night's events to Uncle Ned as they stood around the rig. They told him about all the strange things that had been happening to them since they started investigating.

"Papooses must be careful," Uncle Ned cautioned. "Sometimes bad people 'round."

"We'll be careful," Mandie promised. "Are you coming on to my grandmother's with us now?"

"No, Papoose. Must go. Horse wait under tree." He waved his hand toward a horse tethered under a bare tree across the cobblestoned street. "I come again. Remember—Papoose must think," he said. "Always think first, then do things."

"I'll try to remember that, Uncle Ned," Mandie promised.

"I promise Jim Shaw when he go to Happy Hunting Ground that I watch over Papoose, but Papoose must learn to watch, too," the old Indian reminded her.

"I love you, Uncle Ned," Mandie said, rising on her tiptoes to give him a quick hug. "I'll be careful."

Uncle Ned hugged Mandie in return, then hurried across the street to his waiting horse.

The young people piled into the rig. Ben picked up the reins, and they waved to the old Indian as he mounted his horse and rode away.

When the rig started off, Celia looked up at the clock in the steeple. "It's twenty minutes till eleven!" she exclaimed.

Mandie frowned at Joe. "I don't remember hearing the bells ring while we were in the church," she said, "but I know we got there before ten o'clock."

"You're right. They didn't ring," Joe said with a puzzled look on his face.

"No, they didn't," Celia agreed.

"More and more mystery," Mandie said. "We've just got to solve this thing before forty-'leven hundred more things happen."

"Well, right now I imagine your grandmother and my father are beginning to wonder where we are," Joe told her.

"I know," Mandie said. She was more worried about going back to face the adults than she was about all that had happened to them that night.

# Chapter 7 / Back to School

Mrs. Taft and Dr. Woodard sat waiting in the parlor when the young people returned from the church.

Hurriedly hanging their coats on the hall tree, the three went to sit on stools near the blazing fire. They were cold from the weather and the fright they had just had as well as from the ordeal of now relating their adventure to the adults. Mandie picked up Snowball, who was curled up asleep on the hearth rug, and began to pet him.

Mrs. Taft had Ella serve hot cocoa. She and Dr. Woodard listened without interrupting as the three told of the events of the night. They raised eyebrows and gasped at some parts of the story but waited until the young people had finished. Then Mrs. Taft scolded them.

"I'm sorry, Grandmother," Mandie said, "but we didn't intentionally get locked in."

"No, I don't suppose you did," Mrs. Taft answered. "However, I shall have to speak to Ben. He should have stayed right with you all."

Dr. Woodard cleared his throat. "That could have been an unsavory character who locked you in," he said. He turned to Mrs. Taft. "Do you think they should just stop all this investigating business?"

"Oh no, please!" Mandie pleaded. "We have to find out what's going on."

Mrs. Taft thought for a moment. "I suppose it would be all right if they only go in the daytime—and if Ben stays right with them. But no more night adventures."

The three young people looked at each other.

"I won't be here tomorrow night anyway," Joe conceded. "We have to go home after church tomorrow."

"And we have to go back to school tomorrow afternoon," Celia added.

"We may not have time to do anything else about the mystery now, anyway," Mandie said with a sigh.

"It's late now," Mrs. Taft said. "You all get upstairs to bed. Tomorrow is Sunday, and we all have to get up early and go to church."

The young people started to leave the room and Snowball followed.

Mandie turned quickly and ran back to Dr. Woodard. "We've been so wrapped up in what happened to us that we forgot to ask about Hilda," she said. "How is she, Doctor Woodard?"

"About the same. No better. No worse," he replied.

"Is she going to just stay that way?" Mandie asked. "Isn't she ever going to get better?"

"We hope she will, Amanda," Dr. Woodard replied. "Like I said before, it's up to the Lord."

Mandie turned to the others. "Don't forget Hilda in your prayers tonight," she said.

Early the next morning, everyone was up, rushing around to get ready for church. At breakfast, Dr. Woodard announced that there was still no change in Hilda's condition. The nurses remained at her bedside around the clock, but Mandie felt frustrated that no visitors were allowed.

As they all piled into the rig to go to church, Mrs. Taft spoke quietly to the driver. "Ben, I need to have a little talk with you some time this afternoon," she said.

"Yessum, Miz Taft." Ben looked nervous.

Mandie leaned forward to whisper in his ear. "Don't get so worried," she said. "It's nothing really bad."

Without a reply, Ben picked up the reins and drove sedately to the church. He always left Mrs. Taft at her church and then drove on to his own down the road, picking up Mrs. Taft again after services were over.

As the group stepped down from the rig, Mrs. Taft looked back at her driver. "Now, please don't be late, Ben," she said. "We're in a hurry today."

"Yessum, Miz Taft," Ben answered, muttering to himself as he drove off.

Once inside the church, they all went to their Sunday school classes. Mrs. Taft's was at the rear of the main floor, and Dr. Woodard visited the men's class in a side room nearby. As the young people headed down to the basement for their classes, the first thing they noticed was the doorknob securely fastened to the door at the bottom of the stairs.

"I can't believe my eyes!" Mandie exclaimed in a whisper.

"It seems that whoever is doing these things around here comes back to reverse whatever happened," Joe remarked. "First the *Help!* banner and now this doorknob...."

"Maybe the person is sorry afterward," Celia suggested.

"They're going to be sorry when we finally find them out," Mandie promised. "The house of the Lord is no place to play games like this."

Celia and Joe agreed.

After Sunday school, the young people went upstairs and joined Mrs. Taft and Dr. Woodard in the family pew for the preacher's message. Mandie was happy that the two big stoves in the sanctuary were roaring with fires to warm the whole room. *How different from last night*, she thought.

As soon as Reverend Tallant stepped up behind the pulpit, he mentioned the mysterious goings-on in the church. "We have not been able to remove the writing from the back wall of the church yet, but we should have that accomplished tomorrow," he began. "Now, however, we have another complaint. It seems that neighbors living nearby heard the organ playing here in the sanctuary along about midnight. Someone notified the sexton, Mr. Clark, and he came down, looked around, and found nothing."

The minister paused momentarily while latecomers were being seated. "Mr. Clark said he had gone through and locked the door at ten o'clock," Rev. Tallant continued. "Everything was all right then."

The three young people looked at each other.

"Ten o'clock?" Mandie whispered. "He certainly didn't check the basement then because we were locked in down there before ten, and it was twenty minutes to eleven when we got out."

Celia nodded.

"You don't know what time we got locked in," Joe whispered. "The bells didn't ring at ten o'clock, remember?"

Dr. Woodard nudged his son and shook his head.

The young people hushed.

The preacher continued speaking. ". . . and we want to ask for your prayers for little Hilda Edney, who is living with Mrs. Taft. She is very ill with pneumonia. Mrs. Tillinghast and her sister, Miss Rumler, also need our prayers at this time. They are both quite sick with the flu. Now let us pray."

Mandie bowed her head with the rest of the congregation and joined in the prayers, especially for Hilda. She was worried about her. Dr. Woodard had to leave for home after dinner, and although there were other doctors in Asheville, she trusted her friend Dr. Woodard more than them all.

At the conclusion of the service, Ben waited for them as they shook hands with the preacher at the door and stepped out onto the porch.

On the way home, the young people discussed the newest development in the church mysteries.

"So someone was playing the organ at midnight," Mandie said, trying to make some sense of it. "Well, I'd like to know how anybody got inside the church. It was all locked up when we left."

"Maybe they were able to open the window where Uncle Ned removed the bars," Joe reasoned. "Come to think of it, the preacher didn't mention that someone had torn the bars off that window."

Mrs. Taft spoke up. "That's because I spoke to him before he preached and told him what happened to y'all last night," she explained. "And I promised him I would pay for the damage."

"So, since he knew who did it, he didn't mention it," Mandie said. Suddenly she caught her breath in alarm. "I hope he doesn't think we've been doing all those other things."

"Of course not, Amanda," her grandmother assured her. "But I did tell him that y'all were trying to solve the puzzle for him."

"You told him what we were doing?" Mandie gulped.

"What else was I to say when the damage was there?" Mrs. Taft replied. "It had to be explained some way."

"You're right, Grandmother," Mandie agreed. "I hope he doesn't mind our getting involved."

Mrs. Taft smiled. "I'm sure no one will mind if y'all are able to solve this mystery," she said.

Ben pulled the rig up in front of Mrs. Taft's house and helped her from the vehicle.

As the others climbed down, Mrs. Taft spoke to the driver again. "Come to the back sitting room in about two hours, Ben," she instructed. "The doctor and Joe will be leaving as soon as we finish dinner, and then the girls have to return to school. I want to talk to you before you take them back."

"Yessum, Miz Taft," Ben replied, stepping back into the rig to move it from the front driveway. "I'll be dere."

Inside the house, Dr. Woodard headed upstairs to check on Hilda while everyone else sat in the parlor, waiting for dinner to be put on the table. Mrs. Taft was strict with her servants on Sunday. She insisted that they attend their churches, and all the cooking for Sunday was done on Saturday so that when the cook came home from church, all she had to do was warm everything and put it on the table.

Mrs. Taft sat in a big overstuffed chair in the parlor and looked lovingly at her granddaughter. "Do you and Celia have your things together to take back to school, dear?" she asked.

"Yes, ma'am," Mandie replied. "We're all ready. Are you going to send for us again next Friday?"

"If you and Celia want to come, of course, dear," Mrs. Taft answered. "You know I am always glad to have you girls here with me anytime."

"Thanks, Grandmother," Mandie said. "I'm always so happy to get out of that school, and I imagine Celia is, too."

Celia nodded.

"Especially when there's some kind of adventure going on," Joe teased.

Mandie pretended to look hurt. "You won't be able to come next weekend, will you?" she asked.

"Not unless my father has to come back," he said.

Dr. Woodard entered the room. "I still don't see any change in Hilda," he said. "I've changed the treatment a little, and I hope that will make a difference. But for now, she's just not making any progress."

"Oh, Dr. Woodard, couldn't I just open the door and peek in?" Mandie begged.

"No, I'm sorry, Amanda," he replied. "You will all have to stay away from her room for the time being."

"Will you be coming back next weekend to check on her?" Celia asked.

Mandie's eyes brightened as she looked at Joe, awaiting the answer.

"I'm not sure," Dr. Woodard said. "We'll see."

Mandie smiled at Joe. *At least he didn't say no*, she thought.

As soon as the noon meal was over, Dr. Woodard and Joe left in their buggy. Mrs. Taft retired to the back sitting room to talk to Ben.

Mrs. Taft told the Negro man to sit down. "Now, Ben, I want to know why you didn't stay right with Miss Amanda and her friends when you took them to the church last night," she began.

"I stayed in de rig, Miz Taft," Ben replied.

"But you fell asleep in the rig, and those young people were locked in the church," she scolded. "If Uncle Ned hadn't come along when he did, there's no telling when they would have gotten out."

"But, Miz Taft," Ben replied. The girls could hear him scuffing his feet nervously. "You see, it's like dis heah—I ain't s'posed to go in white folks' church."

"That's nonsense, Ben, and you know that," Mrs. Taft argued. "You know as well as I do that there's a gallery in that church where the colored people are all welcome to come and join in our services. There's no reason in this world why you can't go inside a white people's church."

"I don't go in dat gallery neither, ma'am," Ben replied. "You go to yo' church. I goes to mine. You white. I'se a Negro."

"You are not obligated to attend church with white

people, Ben, but you are obligated to carry out my instructions," Mrs. Taft said firmly. "That's what I pay you for—to do what I ask you to do. Now I don't want to hear any more nonsense. If you want to keep your job, you'll have to do whatever the job requires. Is that understood?"

"I understands, Miz Taft," Ben replied. "If you say dat's part of my job, den I does my job next time."

"Thank you, Ben. I knew I could depend on you," Mrs. Taft said. "You know it isn't long until Christmas, and I always give the pay raises at Christmas."

"Yessum, Miz Taft. You sho' does."

"You are not to let the girls out of your sight again when I have left them in your care," Mrs. Taft continued. "Not out of your sight for one minute. Can I depend on you next time they go somewhere?"

"Yessum. Yessum. You kin 'pend on me."

"Thank you. Now get the rig around to the front door," Mrs. Taft said. "It's about time for the girls to go back to school."

"Yessum."

Minutes later, the girls were reluctantly on their way back to school. When they arrived, Ben took their luggage to their room. The girls stopped to speak to Miss Hope, whom they met in the front hallway.

"I hope you young ladies had a nice weekend," Miss Hope said in greeting.

"Yes, ma'am, we did," the girls replied together. "Did you?"

"We've had a little sickness here this weekend," Miss Hope informed them. "Two of the girls came down with flu—Mamie Wright and Betty Blassingame. They both went home. Mamie just lives over in Hendersonville, and Betty lives out in the country near here, so their parents came and got them." Miss Hope looked worried. "I do hope we don't have an epidemic here in the school."

"Hilda has pneumonia. She's real bad off," Mandie told her.

"Oh, dear, I'm sorry," Miss Hope replied. "I'll be praying for her, and I'll pray that you two don't come down with it."

"Thank you, Miss Hope," the girls said.

"Hurry along, now, and get freshened up for supper," the schoolmistress told them as she continued down the hall.

As soon as the girls were sure she was out of sight, they took the steps, two at a time, up to their third-floor room.

"Well, I guess it's all lessons until Friday," Mandie said, pushing open the door to their room.

Celia followed, and both girls quickly removed their coats and bonnets and started to lay them on the bed. Instantly they jumped back and screamed.

There in the middle of the bed, on top of the counterpane, lay a dead mouse!

At the sound of their screams, Miss Prudence, who had been walking by, jerked the door open. "What are you—?" She saw the mouse, turned pale, and without a word slammed the door, running down the hallway, calling for Uncle Cal.

Mandie and Celia backed away from the bed and stood frozen there in terror.

"Sh-she's afraid of m-mice, too," Mandie managed to say.

Celia moved toward the door. "I'm g-g-getting out of here," she said, backing out of the room.

In seconds Uncle Cal appeared with a garbage bucket and a brush in his hand. "Where dat so-an'-so mouse, now, Missy?" the Negro man asked. He spotted it at once. Quickly turning the bucket sideways, he brushed the dead mouse inside. "All gone, now, Missy," he announced as he headed out the door.

Mandie's heart was pounding. "Oh, thank you, Uncle Cal," she said. "Thank you."

As he went out the door, Aunt Phoebe hurried in, carrying a clean bedspread. She quickly pulled off the one on the bed and replaced it with the one she had brought.

Mandie still trembled with fright. "Aunt Phoebe, do you suppose that's the mouse we found in the chifferobe?" she asked shakily.

Celia came back inside the room to hang up her coat.

"I don't be knowin', Missy," the old Negro woman said, smoothing the wrinkles out of the fresh counterpane. "But I tells you one thing. Miss Prudence, she be knowin' now dat mouse was real!"

"And Miss Prudence was afraid of it, too, just like us," Celia added.

"I hope she does something about it," Mandie said. "I think someone put that thing on our bed, and I hope we find out who did it."

"We find out," Aunt Phoebe promised.

## Chapter 8 / More Trouble

Days passed slowly that week for Mandie and Celia at school. They longed for Friday to come so they could return to Grandmother Taft's and continue their investigation of the mystery.

The newspaper had declared a flu epidemic in the town of Asheville. Hundreds of people were ill, and the people in the town were blaming it on the mysterious happenings at the church. The bells continued ringing thirteen at midnight and the wrong number of rings at other hours during the day.

By Thursday of that week over half of the school had come down with the flu.

Miss Prudence addressed the students at breakfast on Thursday morning. "Young ladies," the headmistress began, looking around at the girls as they stood behind their chairs, "as you know, many of our students have contracted that dreadful flu that is going around town. We don't want it to spread any further here if possible. Therefore, classes will be dismissed until the epidemic is over."

The girls all looked at each other. It was unheard of for any of the students to speak out without being asked, but this particular morning Mandie forgot about the rules and dared asked a question. "Does that mean we can all go home, Miss Prudence?"

The headmistress looked sharply at Mandie, and Mandie cringed.

"Amanda, you have not asked permission to speak," the headmistress reprimanded. "However, since we want to get this settled as quickly as possible, I will answer your question. Yes, the girls who live near enough to come back at short notice may go home. We believe that you who are not sick are less likely to come down with this illness if you are in your own homes. Does that answer your question, Amanda?"

"Thank you, Miss Prudence," Mandie said. "Then I have permission to go to my grandmother's while classes are out?"

"That is correct," Miss Prudence replied. "But you girls who live a long distance away will have to stay here."

Celia looked at Mandie and without moving her lips, she whispered, "That means I don't get to go home. It's too far."

Mandie kept her gaze on Miss Prudence but muttered under her breath, "You can go to Grandmother's with me. We'll ask."

Miss Prudence continued, "You girls may leave the school as soon as you can make arrangements to go home. Beginning today, there will be no classes until further notice. Now let us give thanks for this food."

After breakfast Miss Prudence gave Celia permission to go with Mandie. The two girls could hardly wait for Uncle Cal to take them to Grandmother Taft's house. Hurrying to their room, they hastily threw things into bags and laid out their coats and bonnets.

"We don't know how long we'll be staying, so I guess we'd better take plenty of clothes," Mandie advised.

"Right," Celia agreed. "I'm sorry those girls are so sick, but this is good luck for us."

"I hope they all get well soon," Mandie said, dropping her school books into a bag. "I think I'll take some of my books so I can study a little now and then while we're at Grandmother's."

"That's a good idea. Then we won't get too far behind," Celia replied. She added some of her own books to her bag. "We'll be having our half-year examinations after Christmas holidays, and that's not very far away. It seems like we've had so many holidays—and now this unexpected time out."

"We're lucky Grandmother lives right here in town," Mandie said. "All we have to do is wait for Uncle Cal to take us. And just think, we'll have a little extra time to work on the mystery."

"We won't have Joe to help us, though," Celia reminded her.

Mandie flopped down on the bed. "Well," she said, "as long as Grandmother lets Ben go with us, we can try to solve something."

"Miss Prudence told us to take our things down to the front hall, remember?" Celia prompted.

Mandie jumped up and grabbed two bags. "We'll have to make two trips," she said.

"If we put our coats and bonnets on, we won't have to carry them, and we'll have two hands free to carry the bags," Celia suggested.

"You're right," Mandie laughed. "I'm in such a hurry, I'm not thinking right."

After putting on their coats and bonnets, the girls picked up two large bags each. They made their way down the stairs to the alcove in the front hallway. Just as they sat down to watch out the window for Uncle Cal, they saw him bringing the rig up the driveway. They grabbed their bags and went outside to meet him.

"Uncle Cal, I sure hope you and Aunt Phoebe don't get that flu," Mandie told the old man.

"I do, too, Missy Manda," he replied, putting the bags in the rig. "We'se too old to git dat kind of sickness. Might be bad. Old people die easier than you young ones."

"Please be real careful, and stay away from the sick ones as much as you can," she said, as she and Celia stepped into the rig.

"We has to he'p, Missy Manda," Uncle Cal said, picking up the reins. "Dat's whut we be heah fo'. Sick folks gotta have he'p, too."

"Maybe Dr. Woodard will come to town and help doctor the sick ones," Mandie said. "Hilda is real sick, according to the note I got from Grandmother yesterday, so he'll probably come back to see her."

True to her prediction, the next day, as Mandie and Celia sat looking out Mrs. Taft's parlor window, Dr. Woodard pulled his buggy up into the front driveway. The girls jumped up and ran to the front door to greet him.

Mandie opened the door. "Oh, Joe!" Mandie exclaimed. "How did you manage to come, too?"

Dr. Woodard followed his son into the front hallway as they exchanged greetings and removed their coats and hats.

"The Swain County schools closed today," Joe explained. "The flu hasn't reached that far yet, but they hope that by closing the schools it won't spread as far if someone comes down with it."

Mrs. Taft came into the hall to greet them. "Do come into the parlor to warm yourself before you go up to see Hilda," Mrs. Taft said to Dr. Woodard.

Joe followed the others into the parlor. Making his way with his father over to the hearth where the fire was blazing, he rubbed his hands together to warm up.

Snowball, curled up asleep on the rug, opened one eye to see who was invading his place at the hearth, then dozed off again.

Mandie sat on a stool near the hearth and looked up

at Dr. Woodard. "Our school is closed temporarily, too," she said. "About half of the girls have come down with the flu."

"I'm glad of that," the doctor replied, turning to warm his back in front of the fire. "Maybe it won't spread anymore."

Mrs. Taft sat down on the settee. "Did you know how bad the epidemic was here?" she asked.

"That's why I came to Asheville," the doctor replied. "To see what I could do to help the local doctors. We're lucky in Swain County. We don't have a single case yet."

"What about in Franklin?" Mandie asked, a little worried. "Is there any flu there?"

"Not that I know of, Amanda," Dr. Woodard replied. "I don't think you have to be concerned about your mother and your Uncle John. The flu all seems to be centered right here in Asheville."

"The newspaper says people are blaming it on the goings-on down at the church," Mrs. Taft told him, "as if that could bring on an epidemic."

"People can get some funny ideas sometimes when they can't figure out what's going on," Dr. Woodard said, sitting down in an armchair nearby.

"We're going to solve the mystery," Mandie announced. "Then they'll know how crazy their idea is."

Mrs. Taft looked at her granddaughter and smiled. "I certainly hope y'all can put an end to whatever's going on, Amanda," she said, "but I think it will take some doing."

Dr. Woodard went upstairs to see Hilda. He returned a short time later, shaking his head. "She's just about the same," he reported. "The nurse said she has been able to force a few spoonfuls of broth down Hilda's throat now and then, and she has been taking water, but she seems to just lie there, unaware of what's going on around her."

The young people planned to go to the church the

next morning. But it didn't work out that way.

Mandie and Celia woke early when Annie crept into the room. Trying not to disturb them, she started a fire in the fireplace. The girls, half asleep, lay there silently until Annie had left and the fire began to warm the room.

"Today's an important day," Mandie told her friend. "Let's get dressed and go downstairs. Joe may be already eating breakfast. He's always so hungry." Jumping out of bed, she reached for her clothes.

Celia stretched for a moment, then followed.

Snowball, who was curled up at the foot of the bed, leaped down to the floor to avoid being covered by the bedclothes the girls threw back. Finding a nice warm place by the fire, he curled up to go back to sleep.

Mandie laughed. "Look at Snowball," she said. "He doesn't want to get up."

"I didn't either," Celia remarked as she hastened into her clothes. "It was so warm in that bed."

When they finished dressing, the girls hurried quietly down the stairs to the breakfast room. Joe was already there, sitting at the table with a huge plate of food in front of him. But what caught their attention was the fact that the opened curtains displayed a heavy downfall of snow.

"Oh, no!" Mandie cried, rushing to look out the window.

"Oh, yes," Joe replied. "It's probably a foot deep out there already, and it just keeps coming."

Celia stood beside Mandie, surveying the white-blanketed outdoors. "We can't go out in that," she moaned.

Mandie turned away from the window to the sideboard where platters of food awaited them. "Maybe Grandmother will let us go out for a little while," she said, helping herself to the food.

"I'm pretty positive she won't," Joe disagreed, hastily eating his food. "She'll be afraid you'll get sick if you roam around in all that snow. Besides, the roads would have to be cleared off before Ben could get the rig through."

When the girls had filled their plates, they joined Joe at the table.

"What about your father?" Mandie asked. "Will he be able to get out to see the sick people?"

"He always does," Joe said. "With all the snow we have in Swain County, he knows how to manage. He leaves the buggy at home and rides his horse. That horse is used to snow, and it's easier to get around on horseback than it is to drive a buggy."

"That's an idea," Mandie said, looking up at the others. "Maybe we could ride some of Grandmother's horses to the church."

Joe looked doubtful. "I'd say that as long as it's snowing, you might as well be content to sit here in the house," he told her. "Your grandmother won't let you go out."

Joe was right. Mrs. Taft firmly told the young people there would be no traipsing around in the snow outside. She didn't want them to get sick. And they could fall and have an accident. She was responsible for Celia, too.

Dr. Woodard strapped his medical bag onto the saddle he borrowed from Mrs. Taft for his horse and carefully made his way around town visiting sick people.

The next day, which was Saturday, was still snowy and cold. The newspaper reported a long list of deaths caused by the flu epidemic. Complaints about the mysterious goings-on at the church filled the paper. People blamed the church for the town's bad luck—first the flu and now the terrible snowstorm. Some even dared suggest that the church be torn down if the members couldn't solve its troubles.

It continued to snow and snow. More and more people continued to fall ill. The young people sat in the house, fussing because they couldn't get at the mystery. Early Sunday, the snow quit, but it was almost waist-deep in places. People were out early trying to shovel the snow off the main streets in town because there were no city employees to do such a job.

One of the preacher's farmhands came by Mrs. Taft's house with the message that Rev. Tallant had come down with the flu, and there would be no service at the church that morning. The church would be unlocked, he said, for anyone wanting to go there and pray, but there would be no service. The young people stood in the kitchen listening as the man talked to Mrs. Taft and drank hot coffee.

As soon as the man left, Mandie asked her grandmother, "Could we all just go to the church, anyway, this morning?"

"Amanda, you can pray here at the house as well as you can at the church," Mrs. Taft told her.

"It's a shame that we let the weather keep us away from the Lord's house," Mandie replied.

"Amanda!" Mrs. Taft scolded. "That's only your attempt to get at the mystery."

Dr. Woodard came through the back door, stomping his feet. He unbuttoned his heavy coat. "Cold out there!" he announced, removing his coat.

"Hurry on in to the fire in the parlor," Mrs. Taft invited, "and I'll get Ella to bring you some hot coffee."

"Did you get through the roads all right?" Mandie asked eagerly.

"Well, yes, the roads are pretty clear," Dr. Woodard said. "And I noticed Ben has even cleared the driveway here. But the snow is piled up higher than my head along the sides of the road. It really snowed!"

Mandie followed her grandmother and the doctor to the parlor as Celia and Joe tagged along behind.

As the adults took chairs by the fire, Mandie sat on a stool nearby. "Grandmother," she said, "Dr. Woodard says the roads are clear. Couldn't we go to the church for a little while? Please?"

"There's no service this morning," Dr. Woodard told her. "I've just been to Reverend Tallant's. He's a sick man."

"We got that message a little while ago," Mrs. Taft said. She looked over at Mandie. "I suppose you may go if Ben goes with you all and stays right by your side. But you must promise to be gone no longer than two hours. We'll be having dinner in a little over two hours."

"I promise," Mandie said quickly. "Thank you, Grandmother."

"Thank you, Mrs. Taft," Celia echoed.

Joe stood next to his father. "Do I have permission to go, too?" he asked.

Dr. Woodard looked at the young people's happy faces. "I suppose so," he said, "but remember what Mrs. Taft told you. Stay right with Ben, and be back within two hours."

The young people hastily grabbed their coats and hats and boots. They had no idea what they would do at the church, but they were eager to get there and look around.

This time Ben stayed with them. Inside the church, he stopped at the back of the sanctuary and looked around.

There was nobody else in the church. Evidently no one had come to pray. The young people searched the church. Ben held his breath as Mandie and Joe scaled the rope ladder to the belfry.

"Lawsy, Missy!" Ben gasped. "Miz Taft'll skin you alive if she ketch you a-doin' dat."

Halfway up the ladder, Mandie called down to him. "She probably did the same thing when she was young."

When they came back down, Ben followed them back into the sanctuary.

"Let's go down into the basement," Mandie suggested.

Ben took a seat in the back pew. "I stays right heah

and watch de front do'," he said. "I lets you know if'n somebody come in dis time."

"That's a good idea, Ben," Mandie called back to the Negro driver as she and the others headed for the basement.

There was no disturbance of any kind down there and no sign of anyone else being around.

The bells started ringing. The young people stopped to count, then ran through the church and up to the belfry. As they got there, the bells gave one last ring.

"It's eleven o'clock," Celia said, following Joe and Mandie to the rope ladder. "And the bells rang twelve."

They again went up into the belfry but could find no sign of anyone having been there.

"Guess we might as well go back to your grandmother's house," Joe said.

"I suppose so," Mandie agreed. "I was hoping we'd find something else here."

In the meantime, Ben, sitting on the back pew, stretched out his long legs to get comfortable and maybe take a nap. The toe of his boot caught in a loose thread in the edge of the carpet runner that ran the length of the pew. The rug was tacked to the floor and he reached down to disentangle his shoe.

"Now whutdat?" the Negro man mumbled to himself, as he felt a lump under the carpet where it had come loose.

He withdrew his boot from the thread and felt along the carpet. Poking under it with one finger he pushed out an old dirty key. Picking it up, he examined it, but he didn't know how to read and there was some kind of writing on the key.

"Oh, well," he said to himself, tossing the key in the air and then putting it in his pocket.

He stretched his legs back out, careful not to disturb the loose carpet. But the young people were there before he had a chance to take a nap.

"We're ready to go, Ben," Mandie told him as they picked up their coats and hats. "We haven't found a thing."

Ben stood up. "Dem bars on dat window, is dey still pulled off?" he asked.

"They're still off," Mandie replied. "Grandmother promised to pay for the damages we did, but she hasn't had time yet to get them fixed, I suppose."

"I s'pose somebody could be comin' and goin' through dat window whilst dem bars ain't on it," Ben told them.

The young people looked at each other.

"You're right, Ben," Joe agreed. "It would be easy to open that spring latch on the window with a knife and then close it back. No one would know it was ever open."

"Well, we can't just sit down there by that window waiting for someone to come in," Celia argued.

"We'll do that later," Mandie said. "Right now, we have to keep our promise to Grandmother and get back."

When the young people returned to Mrs. Taft's house, the place was in an uproar.

Hilda was missing! The house was being searched thoroughly for the girl.

"What happened, Grandmother?" Mandie asked anxiously.

"It seems that the nurse dozed off because she had been on duty since Friday night. The nurse who was to relieve her was unable to get through the snow," Mrs. Taft explained. "When the nurse woke up a while ago, Hilda was gone."

"How long has she been missing?" Joe asked.

"We don't know," Mrs. Taft replied. "The nurse said she must have dozed off some time before daylight, and she didn't wake up until a few minutes ago."

"Oh, please don't let any harm come to Hilda!" Mandie prayed, looking upward as she talked to God.

The young people quickly joined in the search. Every crack and corner of the huge mansion was looked into. Every inch of the grounds and the outbuildings was searched. Hilda was nowhere to be found.

"I don't understand how she got away in the weak condition she's in," Dr. Woodard declared as they all gathered in the parlor. "This could be serious for her, I'm afraid."

The townspeople quickly heard about the missing girl and came to join the search. Hours passed. There was no trace of Hilda anywhere!

## Chapter 9 / Discovery in the Belfry

After going over Mrs. Taft's entire estate without finding Hilda, the search party fanned out all across town.

It was not snowing, but the high drifts, bitter cold temperatures, and strong north wind made things more difficult. Everyone was worried about the condition of Hilda's health.

Mrs. Taft allowed Mandie, Celia, and Joe to go with Ben in the rig to help look for Hilda. They knocked on doors and got permission to search people's yards and outbuildings. As they worked their way through the streets, they found themselves near the church about dusk.

"Ben, let's go look around the church and the grounds while we're this close," Mandie suggested.

"Whatever you says, Missy," Ben agreed, turning the horses in that direction.

"Do you think she could have got this far away from your grandmother's house?" Joe asked.

"Maybe," Mandie replied. "Somebody could have given her a ride in their rig or something."

"If she got a ride, there's no telling where in the world she could be by now," Celia reasoned.

Ben stopped the rig in front of the church. "I jes' stay right heah and waits fo' y'all," he said.

"Oh, no, Ben," Mandie protested as she and the others stepped down from the rig. "Grandmother told you that you were to stay right along with us wherever we go, remember?"

"Yessum," Ben grumbled, as he reluctantly followed them up the steps.

As soon as Joe opened the door, they all felt a great warmth from inside the church. They looked around. Someone had built roaring fires in both the big stoves in the sanctuary.

"I wonder why anyone would want to build fires in here today when there's no church service," Mandie said. "It couldn't have been the sexton. He knew Rev. Tallant wouldn't be here today."

Joe shrugged. "I'm not surprised at anything that goes on in this church now," he said.

"Maybe someone came here to pray, and got cold, and decided to build the fires," Celia suggested.

Ben plopped down in the back pew. "Now, y'all go ahaid and do whatever it is you gwine do," he said. "I sits right heah."

"Well, all right," Mandie said. "We're going to search the church for Hilda. If anyone comes in or goes out, yell for us."

"I will, Missy," Ben promised. He stretched his long legs out to get comfortable as he slid down a little in the seat.

"Upstairs first," Joe suggested, leading the way to the gallery.

They looked carefully in every place where someone could possibly hide. By this time they knew every nook and cranny of the building.

Joe skimmed the ladder into the belfry. "Nothing up here," he called down to the girls.

"It seems that we never find anyone here, but we always find signs of someone having been here," Celia remarked.

"We'll catch up with someone sometime. We've got to," Mandie said. "It's impossible for anyone to keep on doing things here and not be caught."

Joe slid down the ladder, and they went back downstairs. Making their way down the side aisle, they went through the door to the classrooms.

"We can go faster if we split up," Joe told them. "You girls take the rooms on that side, and I'll go down this side."

When they found nothing there, they went on downstairs to the basement. But a quick search of all the classrooms there revealed nothing.

"I guess we'd better get going," Joe said, looking around the hallway. "We've covered the whole church except for the pastor's study, and it's still locked."

"Let's go outside and look around the grounds," Mandie suggested.

When they got back to the sanctuary, Ben had nodded off. They all laughed.

Suddenly Mandie heard something. "What was that?" she whispered, looking around quickly.

"Sounded like something moving," Joe said softly.

"It wasn't very loud, whatever it was," Celia observed.

Moving over to the center aisle, they looked around and then started up the aisle. The two big stoves standing in the middle aisle still roared away with their fires.

As they started to walk by the first stove, Mandie glanced down to the right. "Look!" she exclaimed, stooping between the pews.

Joe and Celia huddled behind her to see. There lay Hilda, all wrapped up in choir robes and a small rug.

"Hilda! Hilda!" Mandie cried, smoothing back the girl's tangled dark brown hair.

Hilda didn't move. She looked as though she were soundly asleep.

"Is she—is she—all right?" Celia asked nervously.

Joe bent down and reached for the girl's wrist. "She's alive, but just barely, I believe," he said. "And she does have a terrible fever."

"Ben! Come quick!" Mandie yelled.

Startled, Ben jumped to his feet. "Yessum, yessum, Missy," he answered. Rubbing his eyes, he quickly looked around.

"Down here, Ben," Joe called to him.

Ben hurriedly joined them and gasped when he saw Hilda lying there, so flushed and motionless.

"Quick, Ben," Joe said. "Help me get Hilda into the rig. We've got to get her back to Mrs. Taft's house and into bed fast!"

"Oh, dear Lord," Mandie prayed, "please let Dr. Woodard be there when we get back."

As Joe and Ben picked up Hilda—robes, rug, and all—the girl started mumbling with her eyes closed. "God has come," she said in a whisper. "God has come!"

Tears came to Mandie's eyes. "She's still able to speak," she cried.

The girls followed as Ben and Joe carried Hilda outside and carefully tucked her into the rig.

"This time I give you permission to drive as fast as you can," Mandie told Ben.

"Cain't go too fast, Missy," Ben replied, picking up the reins. "It be slicky on de road 'cause of de snow."

In spite of the roads, however, Ben did manage to get up some speed, and soon pulled up in Mrs. Taft's driveway.

Mandie jumped down and ran to the house. "Grandmother!" she yelled, pounding on the door.

Ella quickly opened the door, and Mandie ran right past her. "Grandmother!" she screamed. "Dr. Woodard! Come quick. We've found Hilda!"

Mrs. Taft and Dr. Woodard hurried into the hall from the parlor just as Ben and Joe were carrying Hilda into the house. Dr. Woodard directed them upstairs, and the nurse who was still there tucked the girl into bed. The young people excitedly explained where they had found her.

Mrs. Taft and Dr. Woodard listened in amazement. Then Dr. Woodard sent everyone out of the room so that he and the nurse could tend to Hilda.

"We might as well go downstairs to the parlor by the fire," Mrs. Taft told the young people. "And you still haven't even taken off your coats and hats."

The young people followed Mrs. Taft down the stairs, unbuttoning as they went. In the front hallway, they hung their coats on the hall tree, then headed into the parlor.

"At least one trip to the church did some good," Mandie remarked as they pulled stools up in front of the fire.

Snowball, who was sleeping on the rug, stretched, stood up, and jumped into his mistress's lap.

Mrs. Taft sat down in an armchair. "I can't imagine how Hilda got there," she said. "And who could have built those fires and wrapped her up in all those things?"

"Someone must have," Mandie answered. "I don't think she could have."

"I hope she's going to be all right," Celia said.

"My father will do all he can. You know that," Joe assured her. "Maybe that warm fire and all those things covering her helped."

"Grandmother," Mandie said. "Hilda kept whispering, 'God has come. God has come.' She didn't open her eyes, and she didn't even seem to know she was being moved."

"She's running a high fever, and I'm sure she's delirious, dear," Mrs. Taft explained. "We'll just have to wait for Dr. Woodard to come back down and tell us how she is."

After a while the doctor joined them in the parlor.

"She's really sick," he said. "She seems to be out of her head completely."

"Let's pray for her," Mandie suggested. "God can heal her."

After they had all prayed for Hilda's recovery, they sat talking in the parlor. Dr. Woodard made repeated trips upstairs to check on the girl.

Mrs. Taft asked Annie, the upstairs maid, to relieve the nurse if she had to leave Hilda's room for any reason. She also instructed the nurse to check all the windows in Hilda's room to be sure they were locked and all the draperies drawn.

The young people talked with Mandie's grandmother long into the night. They still had no real clues in the bell mystery, and now they had Hilda to worry about. They even wondered if there could be any connection between Hilda's running away and the mysterious goings-on in the church, though it didn't seem possible.

There was no change in Hilda's condition that evening. Everybody finally got so sleepy that Mrs. Taft ordered them all to bed. Dr. Woodard promised to sleep in the room across the hall from Hilda's so he would be close in case of an emergency.

Mandie felt as though she had just gone to bed when she heard Annie steal softly into the room where she and Celia were sleeping.

As Annie knelt at the fireplace arranging the kindling for the fire, Mandie sat up and pulled the covers around her. "How is Hilda, Annie?" she asked.

Celia woke and accidentally kicked Snowball, who was sleeping at their feet on top of the quilt.

"Still de same," Annie replied. "I'se jes' been in de room to tend to de fire, and she jes' layin' still. Ain't movin' at all."

Celia sat up beside Mandie in the bed. "At least she isn't any worse then," she said.

Annie moved backward a little and fanned the fire with her big white apron to get it going.

Snowball stretched and yawned, then jumped down to take his place by the warm hearth.

Annie started to leave the room. "Yo' grandma and de doctuh, dey be in de breakfus' room," Annie informed them.

"Joe isn't up yet?" Mandie asked.

"Ain't seen him," Annie replied. "I gotta git his fire goin' now." She went out the door.

Mandie jumped out of bed. "Come on. Let's get dressed," she said. Celia followed.

The two girls shivered a little in the cold room. They quickly grabbed their clothes and stood in front of the fire to get dressed.

Snowball followed them downstairs to the breakfast room. Joe was already there.

As they went to the sideboard, Mandie whispered to Celia, "It takes a girl longer to get dressed than it does a boy."

Celia smiled.

The girls were glad to see the sun shining brightly through the windows where the curtains were pulled back. After exchanging morning greetings with Joe and the adults, Mandie and Celia filled their plates and joined the others at the table.

"I was just in to see Hilda before I came downstairs," Dr. Woodard reported, "and I'm afraid she's still not doing well at all."

The conversation turned to how the young people had found her at the church and questions about the whole puzzling situation.

"Grandmother, could we go back to the church this morning?" Mandie asked. "I'd like to see if the fire's burned out and if there's any sign of anyone there."

Mrs. Taft smiled at her granddaughter. "Amanda, you

visit that church more than you visit with me," she said. "But then, I was the one who got you started in all this tomfoolery. I guess it would be all right for you to go as long as Ben goes with you."

"Thanks, Grandmother," Mandie replied.

"I suppose your school will send someone to let us know when they open back up," Mrs. Taft said.

"I don't believe they'll open up again any time soon. All the girls who didn't go home are sick in bed now," Dr. Woodard said. "I was there yesterday, and the only ones walking around were Miss Hope and Miss Prudence."

"What about Uncle Cal and Aunt Phoebe?" Mandie asked quickly.

"Oh, yes, they're all right," the doctor said.

"Well, I guess we'll have a little longer, then," Celia said.

"But we'd better use what time we have, or we'll never get this mystery solved," Joe reminded them. "You know, I have to leave when my father does."

"That won't be for some time yet son," Dr. Woodard said. "I'd say about two-thirds of the town is down with the flu."

"You young people be sure to wrap up good and wear your boots," Mrs. Taft cautioned them. "I don't want y'all getting sick."

As soon as they finished their breakfast, the young people hurried to the front hallway and put on their coats and hats. Snowball followed them and sat on the arm of the coat tree, watching.

Mandie picked him up. "I'm going to take Snowball with me this time," she decided. "He needs some fresh air."

"I sure hope he doesn't run away," Joe said warily.

Snowball seemed to be thankful to his mistress for allowing him to go. He stayed on her lap in the rig and then clung to her shoulder when they got to the church.

Inside the sanctuary, both stoves were cold. The fires had long since gone out.

Ben dropped into the back pew for his usual nap while the young people looked around. They left their coats and hats on a pew near him.

They checked all the basement classrooms and found nothing there. Then they went up into the gallery and opened the door to the belfry.

"I have an idea," Mandie said, balancing Snowball on her shoulder. "Why don't we all go up into the belfry and just stay there a while? If we're real quiet, we'll be able to hear anything that goes on, and we can watch out the windows up there for anyone coming in or out of the church."

"That's a good idea," Joe said, reaching for the rope ladder. "I'll go first. Then you come next, Celia, so I can help you off at the top. Mandie has done it so much, I don't think she needs any help."

"Well—" Celia hesitated. "I suppose I can go up if that ladder doesn't swing too much."

"I'll hold on to it by the last rung down here to steady it," Mandie promised.

Celia nodded, and Joe scrambled up the ladder, waiting at the top while Celia slowly and cautiously made her way up and Mandie held the bottom rung.

"Just don't look down, Celia," Mandie reminded her. "Keep looking up at Joe."

Celia was shaking so badly that she didn't answer. When she finally got to the top rung, Joe took her hands and swung her up into the belfry. She sat down on the floor quickly. "Oh, my legs feel weak," she gasped.

Mandie hurried after her with Snowball clinging to her shoulder. About halfway up, the kitten looked down and dug his claws into the shoulder of Mandie's heavy dress. Suddenly, he jumped off her shoulder onto the rope ladder and clawed his way up by himself. At the top, he jumped into the belfry and landed at Celia's feet.

Celia laughed nervously. "I guess I'm not the only one who is afraid of that ladder," she said, cuddling the kitten.

"Let's walk around and look outside," Mandie said as she reached the top.

Just then the bells began ringing. The three young people instantly covered their ears at the deafening sound and began counting the rings. Snowball darted about in fear.

"Eleven rings," Mandie said, uncovering her ears. "But it's ten o'clock." She reached down to pick up Snowball.

"And we stood right here watching," Joe said with a puzzled look on his face. "We know that no one else was up here ringing those bells."

Celia made her way over to the walkway around the belfry. "I thought we were going to watch outside," she said.

"We are," Mandie agreed. "I'll go over on this side, and Joe, you take that side over there. There are only three of us, and there are four sides to the steeple, but we can all watch the side where the ladder is."

They did as Mandie suggested. As Joe made his way to the other side, Snowball ran ahead of him and into an almost invisible thread of some kind. It broke.

"Look!" Joe cried, stooping to inspect the thread.

Mandie and Celia watched as he traced the piece of thread to the mechanism of the huge clock. He pulled at it, and it came free, holding a tiny magnet on the end. The girls joined him and all three excitedly examined it. At last they had a clue!

"Someone must have put that magnet on the clock to mess up the mechanism, but where did the string go from there?" Mandie asked, looking around for the other end.

They searched and searched but could not find the

other piece of thread. Nor could they figure out where it had been attached. Finally they sat down on the floor, and Snowball curled up in Mandie's lap.

"Let's just have a quiet thinking session for a few minutes," Mandie suggested.

They all became silent and did not move. Even Snowball sat quietly, content in his mistress's company.

"Why didn't we find this thread before when we were up here, and why didn't all those people who examined the clock mechanism find the magnet before?" Celia asked.

"Maybe whoever put it there took it down whenever they heard somebody coming," Mandie reasoned. "But where could they be hiding?"

They were silent again.

Mandie's sharp eyes caught the slight movement of a panel in the wall. At first she thought she was seeing things, but as the panel moved, she got a quick glimpse of a pair of eyes staring right at her. She caught her breath and froze.

Joe and Celia looked toward the wall to see what had startled her.

Instantly, Joe jumped up and grabbed the moving panel. "Come on out, whoever you are!" he demanded, yanking at the piece of wood.

The girls jumped up to help. Snowball scrambled onto the floor. Joe reached behind the panel and grabbed hold of someone's shoulder.

At first the person struggled, but then he gave up. "I'm coming out," said a man's voice.

"All right. Then get out fast," Joe ordered, still holding on to the panel of wood to keep it from being pushed back into place.

Slowly, from behind the paneling, a little, old, gray-looking man appeared. He fell on his knees in front of the three young people. "I'm sorry, so sorry!" he muttered.

## Chapter 10 / Phineas Prattworthy

The three young people stared in amazement at the gray-haired man before them. He was clean and neatly dressed, but his coat was threadbare.

"Who are you?" Joe demanded.

"Are you the one who has been making the bells ring wrong and doing all those other things around this church?" Mandie asked, putting her hands on her hips.

The old man cowered in front of them.

"Get up," Joe demanded. "We're not going to hurt you."

The man didn't obey. Joe got hold of his shoulders and pushed him backwards so they could see his face. The man was frightened.

He had bushy gray hair, bushy gray eyebrows, a long, thin face, a long nose and a wide mouth with thin lips. His ears stuck out instead of being flat against his head. He looked to be very old and very starved. He blinked at the three of them as tears came into his gray eyes.

"How did you get behind that paneling?" Mandie asked.

"I think you'd better give us some explanations real fast," Joe told the man.

The man's lips quivered as he tried to speak.

Mandie began to feel sorry for him. "Why don't we all sit down and talk," she suggested.

The young people sat down on the floor in front of the stranger who was still on his knees.

"I-I need someone to help me," the man said uncertainly.

"Help you do what?" Mandie asked as Snowball climbed into her lap.

"I am in great trouble that is not my fault," the man replied, clasping his hands tightly.

"I'll say you're in trouble," Joe said. "Just wait until the town gets hold of you."

Mandie looked at Joe with a frown. Then she looked back at the stranger. "Why have you been messing with the bells and doing all those other things?" she asked. "You *are* the one responsible for the *help* banner on the altar, and the writing on the church wall, aren't you?"

"And tearing up the paneling to hide behind," Celia added.

"I'm sorry. I'm sorry," the man said, hanging his head. "What else can I say?"

"Who are you, and where do you live?" Joe asked.

"My name is Phineas Prattworthy," the stranger replied, choking back the tears. "I live way out yonder over the mountain."

"Then why are you hanging around the church? What are you trying to do?" Joe sounded exasperated.

"I can only explain if you promise to help me," Phineas replied.

"We can't promise to help you until we know what you've done," Mandie said.

"But I didn't do what they think I did," Phineas told them, his eyes still wet with tears. "I have been wrongly accused."

Mandie leaned forward and asked, "Accused of what?"

"The grocer down on Main Street thinks I stole some groceries from him," Phineas replied. "But I didn't. I saw the man who did it, though. He came out of the store so fast that he dropped an apple. I picked it up, and when the grocer saw me with it in my hand, he thought I was the man who stole it, but I got away before he could catch me."

"That wasn't very smart," Joe said, shaking his head. "Why didn't you just explain to the grocer what happened?"

"I tried to, but he wouldn't listen. He didn't believe a thing I said," Phineas explained.

"So you came here to this church and started doing all these crazy things?" Joe asked. "Why?"

"I was only trying to get help," Phineas said. "I waited and waited, hoping to attract someone who looked like they would help me, but no one came along who looked trustworthy." He sniffed. "This church is the only place I could find to hide in, out of the cold."

Mandie's heart went out to the man at the thought of him being so hungry and cold. "If you live over on the mountain, why didn't you just go back home?" she asked.

"I lived with my son, and he died last month," Phineas explained. "I don't have any way to make a living. We don't own the house, and with my son gone, there was no one to pay the rent or buy groceries." Nervously, he rubbed the side of his long, thin face. "I'm not begging, mind you. I'd starve to death before I'd beg for something to eat. I'm only asking for someone to help me straighten out this matter with the grocer."

Mandie reached out and took the man's hand. "Mr. Phineas, we'll help you," she promised. "I believe what you've told us. We'll see that you have a warm place to stay and some food to eat."

"Mandie!" Joe exclaimed. "You can't make promises like that. We don't know this man. We'll have to check out his story."

"But he's hungry, Joe," Celia defended Mandie's decision.

"We can at least take him home to Grandmother and let her help us decide what should be done," Mandie said.

"All right. If you insist," Joe said. "But I've still got a lot of questions." He looked directly at Phineas. "How did you get behind that paneling?"

"I worked a piece loose one day and then found that I could slide down through the wall opening into the attic," the man explained.

"Attic?" Mandie's eyes grew wide. "Does this church have an attic?"

"It certainly does," Phineas replied. "That's where I left my bag."

"We didn't find any attic," Celia remarked.

"The only other way you can get into it is through the scuttle hole in the ceiling of the gallery," Phineas told them.

"So that's why we could never catch up with you," Mandie reasoned. "You hid in the attic."

The man nodded. "I saw and heard you three come into the church several times. One time I was in such a hurry to get through the paneling I fell all the way through to the attic. It made such a noise and everything shook so, I just knew you girls would find me that day."

The three people quickly looked at each other.

"So that solves that mystery," Mandie said, with a sigh. "And I suppose you wrote on the wall at the back of the church, too."

"I used whitewash which was supposed to be removable but I couldn't wash it off. It just got all blurred instead," Phineas said.

"And you put the magnet on the clock, too, I suppose," Joe said.

"You see, I used to be in the clock business long years ago. I knew I could control the mechanism with a magnet and I could withdraw it whenever I wanted to. I figured someone would come investigating the bells ringing and maybe they could help me but, like I said, I haven't seen anyone who looked trustworthy," Phineas explained with a sigh.

"And you locked us in the basement and then unlocked the door later. And you put that 'Help' banner on the altar and then took it away. Why did you do things and then reverse what you did?" Mandie asked.

"I guess I just had a guilty conscience," the old man said. "I needed help but I decided the altar was not the place to put such a thing so I took it away. And I had been outside the church and didn't realize y'all were in the basement when I locked that door. Then I heard you down there and had to come back and unlock it."

"Well, why were you locking the basement door anyhow?" Celia asked.

"I had thought I could sleep in the pastor's study on his settee that night and I wanted to be sure the basement was locked off in case anyone came prowling around. Then I found out the pastor's door was locked after all," Phineas said. "I hope you will all forgive me."

"But if you've been here hiding all this time, how could you live without any food?" Joe asked.

"Well, to begin with, I had the apple that man dropped, and then I had to look in trash cans," he told them.

Mandie and Celia cringed.

"The restaurant down on Patton Avenue throws out a lot of good food," he explained. "When I discovered that, I just went behind their building whenever I got hungry and helped myself. I don't eat much anyway."

Tears clouded Mandie's eyes to think of this poor man having to eat out of trash cans! She jumped up, dumping Snowball onto the floor, and grabbed the man's hand to help him up. "Come on," she said. "We're going to my grandmother's."

Joe looked at her with concern. "If you say so," he said.

Phineas seemed to have a bad leg. He was limping.

"Can you get down the rope ladder?" Mandie asked.

"Oh, sure," he answered. "All I have to do is slide."

"I'll go first," Joe offered. He still didn't trust the stranger.

Celia went down next, then Phineas.

As Mandie followed, Snowball fought against going down the ladder. He kept jumping off Mandie's shoulder into the belfry. After three tries, Mandie gave him a little swat and said, "Now you look here, Snowball! We are going down that ladder, and you might as well behave!"

Joe, watching the scene from below, climbed halfway up the ladder and reached for the kitten. "Give him to me," he told Mandie. "I can slide down with one hand."

Snowball squealed with anger as Joe grabbed him and held him tightly in one hand while he made his way down with the other. The kitten squirmed and tried to scratch as Joe landed below.

Mandie jumped off at the bottom and reached for the kitten. "Thanks, Joe," she said.

"Watch out," he warned her. "This cat is mad, and he's trying to scratch."

Mandie held the kitten tightly in both hands. He hushed his loud meowing and cuddled in her arms.

Joe shook his head in disgust, and the young people and Phineas headed downstairs.

As they approached Ben in the sanctuary, the Negro man stood up, looked at the stranger and asked, "Who dat be whut y'all got dere?"

"This is who we've been looking for all this time," Joe answered. "He's the answer to the mystery."

Ben just stood there with his mouth open.

"Come on, Ben," Mandie said. "We're taking him home to Grandmother."

After they were all in the rig, Ben flicked the reins and coaxed the horses to a fast pace. When the Negro driver pulled the rig into Mrs. Taft's driveway, Phineas Prattworthy looked amazed.

"Your grandmother lives here?" he asked.

Mandie climbed down from the rig. "Yes, my grandmother is Mrs. Taft," Mandie explained. "Come on."

Phineas stepped down beside her. "I know who Mrs. Taft is," he said. "I had no idea you were talking about her when you mentioned your grandmother."

"You know her?" Mandie asked, petting Snowball.

The others got down from the rig and stood around, listening.

"I knew your grandfather, Mr. Taft," Phineas told her.

Joe urged them all to go into the house. "I'm cold and hungry," he complained.

Inside, they left their coats in the hallway and ushered Phineas into the parlor where Mrs. Taft sat reading by the fire. Snowball jumped down and ran off down the hallway. Mrs. Taft rose quickly and stared at the man.

Phineas spoke first. "How are you, Mrs. Taft?" he asked, nervously.

"Phineas!" Mrs. Taft exclaimed, hurrying over to greet the man. "It is Phineas, isn't it?"

"Yes, ma'am. I'm Phineas Prattworthy," he replied.

"Where in the world have you been all these years, and where did these young people meet up with you?" Mrs. Taft asked. "Please come and sit down."

Mandie and her friends sat down, speechless, on low stools in front of the fireplace.

Phineas took the chair opposite Mrs. Taft. "Well, I fell on some hard times after y'all left Franklin, and I came over to the mountains to live," he said. "The tax man took all my property."

"You mean you lost that great big beautiful home?" Mrs. Taft looked deeply concerned. "Oh, Phineas, how sad."

"My wife died suddenly with the fever right before we

had to vacate the property," Phineas continued.

"Phineas, I'm so sorry," Mrs. Taft said.

The man fidgeted nervously. "I just had one son, Paul, you know, so he and I rented a small farm up in the Nantahala Mountains. We couldn't make much of a living out of it, but we didn't starve," he said with a weak smile. "Then I had a stroke and was helpless for a long while. I'm not much good anymore. About the time I was beginning to walk again, Paul came down with the flu and died."

"I'm so sorry," Mrs. Taft said again. "But just saying I'm sorry won't help. What can I do for you?"

"Grandmother," Mandie jumped into the conversation, "we found Mr. Phineas hiding in the church. He's the one who has been messing up the bells and everything."

Mrs. Taft looked shocked. "Phineas! You were doing that?"

"Yes, ma'am," he replied. "I'm afraid I'm guilty."

As he retold the story, Mrs. Taft sat staring at him in amazement.

"I can't explain why I did all those strange things at the church," he said. "I just almost went crazy not knowing what to do to get somebody to help me."

"I just can't believe that anyone could accuse you of such a thing," Mrs. Taft exclaimed. "Well, we'll just have to get this all straightened out. I'm well acquainted with Mr. Simpson, the grocer, and I think he'll understand when we tell him the story."

Dr. Woodard joined the others in the parlor after having made rounds in town and checking on Hilda. "Phineas!" he exclaimed in surprise. "How did you get here? The last time I saw you was when I doctored you for that stroke—about a year ago, wasn't it?"

The story had to be told again, and Dr. Woodard listened attentively. When Phineas told the doctor that he didn't know why he did such strange things in the church,

Dr. Woodard looked thoughtful.

"There are a lot of things that can cause a person to behave abnormally," the doctor told him. "Losing your wife, your son, and your house, and having that stroke all in such a short period of time was a lot for a person to bear. And then being unjustly accused and malnourished and living without any heat in that church most of the time—it's no wonder something snapped."

"Then I'm not crazy?" Phineas asked.

"Not likely," Dr. Woodard replied. "I think once we get this thing cleared up and get you well fed and cared for, you'll be back to your old self again."

Mandie smiled at Joe and Celia, satisfied that she had done the right thing in bringing Phineas to see her grandmother.

"That grocer may give you a fight, though," Dr. Woodard added.

Mrs. Taft spoke. "I told Phineas we would get this all straightened out for him. We'll just go talk to Mr. Simpson."

"I'm afraid that won't work, Mrs. Taft," Phineas said. "I tried to talk to him, and he wouldn't listen at all. He has his mind made up and won't change it."

"We'll see that he changes it, won't we, Grandmother?" Mandie said.

"Yes, we will," Mrs. Taft said confidently. "We'll have something to eat in a little while, and then we'll just go visit Mr. Simpson."

Mandie turned to Dr. Woodard. "How is Hilda this morning, Doctor?" she asked.

"I was just upstairs when y'all came in," Dr. Woodard replied. "She is still just lying there. That bout in the snow and the church certainly didn't help her condition."

Mandie explained to Phineas. "Our friend Hilda ran away from here yesterday," she said. "She's a girl my grandmother has living with her. Hilda has been real sick with pneumonia, and then suddenly she disappeared out of her bed. We finally found her in the church late yesterday afternoon. Did you happen to see her?"

"That must be the girl I saw come into the church in her nightclothes," Phineas replied quickly. "She was mumbling something to herself and then lay down on the floor. I thought she went to sleep. I found some old choir robes in a box in the attic and a little rug that was behind the altar, and I tried to wrap her up."

"Are you the one who started the fires in the stoves, then?" Mandie asked.

"Yes," Phineas answered. "It was so cold in the church I was afraid she would die. Then I remembered seeing the woodpile out behind the church, so I just gathered in enough wood and got the stoves going to keep her warm."

"Oh, how can we thank you, Mr. Phineas! You probably saved Hilda's life," Mandie told him.

"Hilda's not right mentally, Phineas," he explained. "And she's always running off somewhere."

"I had no idea who she was, but she looked like she needed help," Phineas agreed.

"The Lord will bless you for your kindness, Phineas," Mrs. Taft said.

"Imagine that," Joe said with a little laugh. "He was the one who covered up Hilda and started the stoves. One more piece of the mystery solved."

Ella came in to announce that the noon meal was on the table.

After a leisurely meal, Mrs. Taft announced that she was going to visit Mr. Simpson, the grocer, and the young people could go with her if they wished.

Mandie, Celia, and Joe excitedly put on their wraps in the front hall.

"After a busy morning tending to the sick, I think I need a couple hours of rest," the doctor said. "And Phineas ought to stay here out of sight until we're sure Mr. Simpson won't cause trouble."

"I'll stay here and soak up some of that warmth from the fireplace if it's all right with you, Mrs. Taft," Phineas added.

Mrs. Taft agreed.

Ben drove the rig sedately down the streets of Asheville. With one hand he kept flipping the key he had found in the church. He had no idea as to what it unlocked, or who had lost it, but somehow the key fascinated him. When he got a chance he would ask Missy Manda to tell him what the writing on it said.

He pulled the rig up in front of Mr. Simpson's grocery store. Mrs. Taft asked him to wait there for them.

Inside the grocery store Mr. Simpson, an overweight, bald-headed man in his middle forties, came forward to greet Mrs. Taft.

"This is a pleasure, Mrs. Taft," he said. "What can I do for you today?"

"We seem to have a problem that I think you can help us with," she replied. Then she explained the situation with Phineas Prattworthy. "He isn't guilty," she concluded.

"Oh, Mrs. Taft, I beg your pardon, but he is," the grocer protested. "Why, he was in here not more than ten minutes ago, stealing canned beans. I saw him."

"Ten minutes ago?" Mandie spoke up. "Mr. Simpson, it couldn't have been Mr. Phineas. He has been with us at my grandmother's house for the last three hours at least."

"That's right," Mrs. Taft confirmed. "We just left him there with Dr. Woodard."

"Please tell me, what does this Phineas Prattworthy look like?" the grocer asked.

"He has a bad leg from a stroke about a year ago, and—" Mrs. Taft began.

"That's the one. He limped," the grocer interrupted.

"I'm sorry, Mrs. Taft, but if you don't bring him in, I'll have to ask the sheriff to come out to your house and get him."

"Oh no, you won't," Mrs. Taft replied angrily. "You are not going to have Phineas Prattworthy arrested—not while he's in my house."

Joe stepped forward. "Mr. Simpson, there is definitely a mistake here," he told the grocer. "Mr. Prattworthy did not steal from you. It must be someone who looks like him."

"I don't have to identify him," Mr. Simpson argued. "I know him by his limp, and he's a stranger in this town."

Several other customers in the store edged closer to listen to the conversation.

"You have caused Mr. Prattworthy much distress by your false accusations. Why, he had to hide in the church to keep you from putting him in jail," Mrs. Taft said.

"Yes, you told me he had been doing all that damage at the church—ringing the bells wrong and writing all over the walls," Mr. Simpson shot back. "That proves that the man is deranged."

The other customers gasped.

"Phineas Prattworthy is not deranged any more than you are, Mr. Simpson," Mrs. Taft snapped. "You drove him to do all those things."

"I can only say that unless you bring him down here first thing in the morning, I'll ask the sheriff to go to your house after him," Mr. Simpson threatened. "Now, I'm sorry, but I have customers to wait on."

"I'll get the best lawyer in the state and sue you for false accusations if you press any charges against Mr. Prattworthy," Mrs. Taft promised. She turned to go. "Just be sure you remember that, Mr. Simpson."

The young people followed Mrs. Taft back out to the rig, Mandie took her grandmother's hand. "You were great in there, Grandmother," she said with admiration. "You handled it just the way I'd have done."

Mrs. Taft smiled and patted Mandie's hand. "I know, Amanda, dear," she said, stepping up into the rig. "You're so much like I was when I was your age."

The young people climbed into the rig.

"Now what are we going to do?" Joe asked as Ben picked up the reins.

"We're going to find the *real* crook," Mrs. Taft replied.

"But how?" Celia asked.

"It was probably some poor farmer around here who didn't have any money to buy food," Mrs. Taft reasoned. "I don't know any other reason a person would steal food from a grocer. I'm not sure how we'll find him, but we will."

When they returned to Mrs. Taft's house, they found Dr. Woodard asleep on the settee in the parlor, but there was no sign of Phineas Prattworthy.

"Sh-h-h!" Mrs. Taft whispered. "The doctor needs his rest. Don't wake him."

After quickly checking the front part of the house, they still couldn't find Phineas.

Annie met them in the hallway and told them what had happened. "Dat man whut was heah," Annie began, "he say tell you, Miz Taft, he have to go find de crook. He say you unnerstan."

Mrs. Taft let out a big sigh. "Thank you, Annie," she said. "I know what he meant." Looking at the young people in disappointment, she said, "Now, why did he do that? The law may very well catch him if Mr. Simpson tells the sheriff who he thinks has been stealing from him. Oh, dear!"

"We'll just have to go find Phineas," Mandie said.

"I doubt that we could find him," Joe remarked. "He's pretty good at hiding."

Annie spoke up again. "Miz Taft," she said, "dat Injun man whut Missy know, he be in de sun room."

"Uncle Ned!" Mandie cried, hurrying to the sun room. "He'll help us find Phineas."

## Chapter 11 / The Robber!

Uncle Ned, as always, agreed to help Mandie and her friends. He knew Phineas Prattworthy and he listened carefully as Mrs. Taft explained the whole story with occasional interruptions from Mandie, Joe, and Celia.

"Must help find," Uncle Ned said as Dr. Woodard came into the sun room.

"Yes, I agree," said Dr. Woodard. "After all, Hilda might have died from the cold if Phineas hadn't done what he did for her."

"But, Dr. Woodard, I don't think he's guilty anyway," Mandie remarked. "We can't let an innocent man be prosecuted."

"Of course not, Amanda," Dr. Woodard replied.

"We find," Uncle Ned assured them. "Go now."

"I know we will find him with you helping us, Uncle Ned," Mandie told the old Indian, as they sat in the warmth from the fireplace. "Grandmother, may we go with Uncle Ned?"

"Amanda I just don't know," Mrs. Taft replied. "Evidently there is a robber involved in this, and he could be dangerous."

"Please, Grandmother," Mandie begged. "We'll stay right with Uncle Ned," she promised.

"Well, I suppose so," Mrs. Taft said uncertainly.

"Thanks," Mandie said.

"May I go, too?" Joe asked his father.

"I suppose if you stay right with Uncle Ned, it'll be all right," Dr. Woodard agreed.

"Thanks Dad," Joe said, grinning.

Mrs. Taft looked at the old Indian. "I'll send Ben with y'all, too," she said. "He can help see that the young people don't get into any trouble."

Uncle Ned nodded in agreement.

"And be back before dark," Mrs. Taft said to the young people.

They all nodded as Uncle Ned motioned for them to go. "Must go while trail fresh," he said.

The young people bundled up and followed the old Indian through the snow with Ben bringing up the rear. Ben didn't seem very happy to be involved in the hunt.

Uncle Ned traced Phineas's tracks in the snow through the yard, into the back, across the surrounding property, and into the main road. There, the tracks disappeared. The snow had been shoveled from the dirt road, and dozens of wagon wheels, horses, and footprints had marked the road.

"Maybe he went back to the church," Mandie suggested.

"He could have," Joe agreed. "We didn't tell Mr. Simpson that he had been hiding in the church—just that he had been ringing the bells and doing all that other crazy stuff. I don't believe Mr. Simpson would look for him there."

Uncle Ned nodded. "We look," he said.

Inside the church, the young people led the way, explaining to Uncle Ned what had happened there. They took him up to the gallery and showed him the rope ladder to the belfry. The old Indian was as agile as the young people as he scaled the rope ladder. Ben refused to go up.

In the belfry, Joe showed Uncle Ned the loose paneling.

"He said he hid in the attic, remember?" Mandie reminded Celia and Joe. "We never did go into the attic. Maybe he's there now."

"How can we get into the attic?" Celia asked nervously.

"He told us he could slide down through the wall behind this loose paneling into the attic," Joe said, shaking the panel in the wall.

Uncle Ned stood there looking and listening. "No other way?" he asked.

"Well, yes. He said there's a scuttle hole in the ceiling of the gallery," Mandie recalled.

"We see." Uncle Ned went back down the rope ladder, and the young people followed.

When they reached the gallery, they found Ben stretched out on one of the benches.

"Big help he is," Joe teased.

Ben got up sheepishly and joined the others.

Uncle Ned immediately spotted the trapdoor in the ceiling, but it was too high for them to reach.

"Need ladder," Uncle Ned said, looking around.

"There isn't a ladder in the building," Joe told him. "We've been through the whole church several times, and I don't remember seeing one anywhere."

"Then we get table, stack, reach," Uncle Ned decided.

The young people understood what the old Indian meant. If they brought the table and chairs up from the basement that they had used to open the basement window, they could probably reach the ceiling.

Ben was put to work helping. It was a job to get the big table up the stairs from the basement and then on up the narrow stairs to the gallery but they finally made it.

Straddling the table over the bench directly under the

scuttle hole, they put a chair on top of the table. The ceiling in the gallery was low. Joe and Uncle Ned could both reach the trap door by standing on the chair.

"I'll go up there," Joe volunteered.

Uncle Ned nodded and stood holding the chair for the boy to step on. The girls held their breaths as they watched. Ben stood back, watching as he flipped the key in his hand.

Joe had trouble trying to slide the trap door open. It refused to budge.

"Get chair. I help push," Uncle Ned told them.

Joe jumped down and hurried to the basement to bring up another chair. He placed it beside the other chair on top of the table.

"Ben, you'll have to hold the chairs this time. Uncle Ned is going to stand up on one and me on the other," Joe told the Negro man.

"All right," Ben agreed. He started to put the key in his pocket as he stepped forward to help. The key slipped out of his hand and went flying between the benches, making a loud rattling noise.

Ben stooped to look around. "I jes' lost day key whut I found in dis chouch de other day."

Mandie quickly asked, "You found a key? In this church? When?"

Ben, down on his knees, looking under the benches, raised his head to answer. "Missy, I find dat key de day y'all make me come inside de church, de fust time. It be on de flo' right under my foot where I set."

Mandie said, "Come on, let's help Ben find his key. He found it here in this church and you remember the man and woman were looking for something they had lost."

The young people quickly covered the floor. Uncle Ned, watching, bent to pick up something at his foot.

"Key," he told the young people, and he handed the key to Mandie.

Mandie squinted to read the faint printing on the key while the others crowded around to see.

"It says *Property of National* something or other, *Charlotte, North Carolina,* I think," Mandie said. "What's that other word there?"

"That's a *k* on the end of the word," Celia determined.

Joe looked closer. "Bank!" he exclaimed. "*Property of National Bank of Charlotte, North Carolina.*"

The girls gasped. Uncle Ned nodded in understanding, but Ben looked confused.

"If dat key be de property of de bank, den I'll jes' send it back to 'em," he said innocently.

"Ben, don't you know what you've found?" Mandie asked. "This must be what the man and woman were looking for here that day we hid behind the curtains."

Celia's eyes grew wide. "And if this is what they lost—"

"Those people must be connected with that bank robbery in Charlotte," Joe interrupted.

"You mean they were bank robbers?" Celia asked.

Mandie looked up at Ben. "Can I keep this key?" she asked.

"Sho', Missy," he replied. "Don't belong to me."

Mandie put the key in her pocket. "Uncle Ned, we need to get in touch with this bank in Charlotte," she said.

"We see, Papoose," the Indian agreed. "Now we go in attic. Be dark soon."

"You're right, Uncle Ned," Joe said, climbing up on one of the chairs. "We have to hurry."

Uncle Ned stepped up on the other chair. Ben held the chairs steady while Uncle Ned and Joe pushed on the trapdoor overhead. After several hard blows, it finally moved, and they were able to slide it back, uncovering a square hole in the ceiling.

Joe swung up inside the hole, and they could hear

him walking around in the attic. "The place is pretty empty," he called down to them. "I see Mr. Prattworthy's bag over there and some odds and ends, but there's nobody up here."

"Come," Uncle Ned called to him. "We go." Joe came back down, and they closed the trapdoor and returned the table and chairs to the basement.

As they left the church, Uncle Ned asked Ben to drive them out of town toward the mountains. "Robber not stay in town. Phinny he go, too," the old Indian decided.

They all nodded. The robber wouldn't want to be seen around town, so he would most likely hide out in the country somewhere. Phineas knew that, too.

As they rode along the bumpy, snow-covered country road, they kept watch for anything unusual. There were very few buildings on the road, a few tumbled-down barns, some rough country houses, an old deserted church building, and a school. They stopped at all these places and quickly searched them.

"Uncle Ned, it's going to be dark soon," Celia reminded him.

"One more place. Then go back," Uncle Ned replied.

"Oh, I do hope we can find him," Mandie said.

"Just hope the robber doesn't find him first," Joe cautioned. "The robber must know what's going on in town."

They came to a narrow dirt road branching off the one they were traveling on. Uncle Ned motioned for Ben to pull up on the side road. "Stop there," he said.

Ben did what he was told and brought the rig to a stop. The side road was too narrow, and the snow was too deep for the rig to go down it anyway.

"Come. We walk," Uncle Ned ordered.

They all piled out of the rig onto the frozen snow.

"What's down this road?" Mandie asked.

"Old ground camp for church," the Indian replied, leading the way.

Mandie laughed. "Oh, you mean a campground for the church."

"No more. Church no more use." Uncle Ned adjusted his bow and sling of arrows on his shoulder.

The young people walked carefully on the frozen snow to keep from sliding down.

Ben trudged along behind them, mumbling to himself. "Dem hosses dey gwine be froze to death 'fo' we gits back," he fussed.

"You put their blankets on them," Joe said. "They'll be all right."

"Not fo' long," Ben argued.

In a little while Uncle Ned stopped for the others to catch up with him. He held up his hand. "Quiet," he said softly. "Not far."

Everyone hushed and cautiously followed the old Indian.

As they came around a curve, a large, old dilapidated building came in sight. Several smaller structures sagged nearby, but no one seemed to be anywhere around.

Again Uncle Ned held up his hand for them to stop. He motioned for them to hide behind a cluster of huge tree trunks nearby, then sniffed the air. "Smoke," he whispered.

There was a loud scuffling noise from somewhere behind the big building. Uncle Ned motioned for them to creep forward and stay out of sight. He slipped around the corner of the building. The noise got louder.

They heard a man's loud voice. "That's what you're going to get for snooping in other people's business," he yelled.

There was a loud crack of a whip.

Uncle Ned took an arrow from his sling and softly crept toward the back of the building. The young people stayed right behind him, and Ben brought up the rear.

As they reached the corner, they saw Phineas. He was sitting, tied up, on the snow-covered ground, and a strange man with a gun strapped to his waist raised a horse whip, ready to strike.

Uncle Ned quickly pulled back his bowstring and let his arrow fly. The arrow whizzed overhead and stuck in the tree trunk just over the stranger's head. The man whirled quickly and reached for his gun, unable to see them hiding around the corner. He looked at the arrow embedded in the tree.

"Indians!" the stranger shrieked.

"These woods are full of Indians, mister," Phineas told him as he wiggled to get free of the ropes. "Great big, strong Cherokee Indians."

"Then we'd better leave," the stranger said anxiously.

In the meantime, Uncle Ned had raced around the building to the opposite corner, and at that moment he shot another arrow above the man's head.

"Looks like they've got us surrounded," Phineas warned. "No way we can get out of here."

"We have to leave," the man insisted, nervously eyeing the second arrow. "Those Cherokee Indians are dangerous."

"You leave. I'll stay right here," Phineas offered. "Those Cherokees are my friends."

"If I leave, you're going with me," the stranger ordered. "And if they're your friends, you can see that no harm comes to us when we leave. Otherwise, you are going to be greatly harmed by me."

Uncle Ned raced back to the corner where the others were watching through the bushes.

The stranger stepped toward Phineas. He had a limp! *So this is the man who stole from the grocer,* Mandie thought. Phineas had found him!

The old Indian motioned for the others to come near.

"I go behind man. Shoot arrow," he whispered. "He turn that way. I run fast. Shoot arrow again other way. Man get all confused."

"What can we do, Uncle Ned?" Joe asked in a low voice.

"You go that way. Get help," Uncle Ned motioned toward a slight path off to the right. "Mumblehead live that way. Two minutes."

Joe understood and nodded his head. Uncle Ned slipped around the building. Joe turned to the path and spoke quietly to Ben on his way. "Stay close to the girls," he whispered. "See that they don't get hurt. I'm going for help."

Ben nodded and moved closer to the girls. Together, they watched the stranger and Phineas through the bushes while Uncle Ned moved all around, shooting arrows from different directions.

The stranger seemed more and more frightened, apparently convinced he was surrounded by a whole tribe of Indians. "Hey, you!" he shouted at Phineas. "Call off these confounded Indians. Tell them we want to leave."

Phineas wiggled on the cold snowy ground to free himself from the ropes that bound him. "Do you think they're going to let us leave when they can see you're my enemy and that you've tied me up like this?" he scoffed. "Don't forget. They're my friends. If you don't release me, they'll come and get you in a few minutes."

The stranger limped around in circles for a while, evidently trying to think of some way out of his predicament. Without a word, he pulled a knife from his belt and slashed the ropes that bound Phineas.

Limbering up his wrists and ankles, Phineas finally managed to stand up. But just then, another arrow whizzed through the air and lodged in the tree behind the stranger, clipping his hat.

"Tell them to let us leave!" the stranger yelled, stomping around on his bad leg.

Phineas looked around and then let out a loud Indian yell as Uncle Ned grabbed the stranger from behind. Suddenly scores of Indians came out of the bushes and surrounded the stranger, taking his gun and knife away from him.

"Thank the Lord!" Phineas shouted. "And thank you, Uncle Ned!"

The girls ran forward and met Joe coming from the other side.

"Go!" an Indian's voice shouted.

The young people looked up to see Ben walking toward them, his eyes wide with fright, and a young Indian brave pushing him forward with an arrow poised at his back.

Ben's legs buckled beneath him, and he fell to the ground, begging for his life. "Please, I ain't done nothin'," he pleaded. "Please!"

Uncle Ned ran to Ben's rescue. "Redbird, leave," he commanded. "Ben friend of Papoose."

Redbird smiled and reached down to help Ben up. Ben rolled away from the young Indian, and managing to get to his feet, he ran to where Mandie and Celia were standing.

Mandie glared at the stranger. "You are the man who stole food from the grocer and caused Mr. Phineas to be blamed for it, aren't you?" she asked as Uncle Ned tied the stranger's hands behind him.

"What are you white folk doing with these Indians?" the stranger asked.

"I'm part Cherokee myself," Mandie answered, "and these Indians are my friends."

Joe stepped forward to help Uncle Ned. "Come on, mister," he said in a deep, important-sounding voice. "We've got a rig not far from here. We're taking you to town."

The stranger protested. "I've got a bad leg," he complained. "I can't walk. Besides, my horse is in that old barn over there."

"You're not riding a horse," Joe ordered. "You'd only run away. You're going in the rig with us."

Uncle Ned called to the oldest Indian there, the head of the group. "Mumblehead, get horse. Tie to rig," he ordered. "Redbird, get braves. Carry bad man to rig. Hurry!"

Mumblehead disappeared while two young Indians stepped forward and picked up the stranger, carrying him to the rig as the others followed. Soon Mumblehead returned with the horse.

"Mr. Phineas, thank goodness we found you in time," Mandie said as they walked along. "Uncle Ned always knows what to do."

"How did you find the man?" Joe asked.

"I watched the store and sure enough, he came back to steal more," Phineas replied. "He stole a bag of beans and escaped before the grocer could catch him, but I followed him. His horse had thrown a shoe, so he was trying to walk," he explained. "He couldn't go very fast. Then when he turned in here off the road, he happened to look back and see me. There weren't enough bushes for me to hide in."

"Weren't you afraid of him?" Celia asked.

"I suppose so, but I was mad, too," Phineas said, "because he was committing crimes I was being blamed for."

"I can see why Mr. Simpson thought y'all were the same person," Mandie commented. "He's short like you, and he has a bad leg."

"Well, we don't exactly look alike," Phineas protested.

They got the stranger safely secured in the rig and tied the horse behind it. Uncle Ned thanked his Indian friends and told them goodbye as he and the others drove off.

The stranger moaned and groaned all the way, and

the young people kept a close watch on him.

Finally Mandie spoke up. "What's wrong with you?" she asked.

"There's lots wrong with me," the stranger replied. "This here leg has got a bullet in it, for one thing."

Mandie gasped. "A bullet?"

"Who shot you?" Joe demanded.

"I guess I might as well come clean, or I'll die from this leg," the stranger said. "My name is Kent Stagrene. I robbed that bank in Charlotte, and the guard shot me," he confessed, beginning to moan again. He bent down to hold his leg; then he looked up. "I got away with the money, though."

Mandie did some quick thinking. Taking the key Ben found out of her pocket, she showed it to the stranger. "Is this the bank?" she asked.

He reached for the key, but she held it back.

"Where did you get that?" Kent Stagrene asked angrily. "That's the key to the strongbox I took."

"Then where is the money?" Joe asked.

"I don't have it anymore," he said, turning pale. "Someone else stole it from me." Within seconds he passed out.

Uncle Ned tapped Ben on the shoulder. "We take stranger to doctor man," he said.

Ben headed for Mrs. Taft's house.

## Chapter 12 / An Angry Mob

By the time Ben pulled the rig into Mrs. Taft's driveway, it was pitch dark.

Ella greeted them at the front door and ran to the parlor. "They's home, Miz Taft, and they's got some man wid 'em," she reported. "Looks like he's hurt."

"Go tell Dr. Woodard," Mrs. Taft ordered, hurrying to the front hallway. "He's up in his room, getting his coat. It's so late that he was about to go out looking for them."

Uncle Ned and Ben carried the still-unconscious man through the doorway. Mrs. Taft stepped back. "Who is that?" she asked shakily. "What's wrong with him?"

"He's been shot," Joe volunteered.

Mrs. Taft began to sway slightly as though she were about to faint.

"We didn't shoot him, Miz Taft," Ben assured her. "Dis de man whut rob de bank in Charlotte. De bank guard done shot him."

Ben and Uncle Ned laid the man on the floor in the hallway.

"A bank robber!" Mrs. Taft cried.

"He need doctor man," Uncle Ned said.

Phineas and the girls gathered around Mrs. Taft.

"Thank goodness, you're back, Phineas," Mrs. Taft said.

Dr. Woodard came hurrying into the hallway, followed by Ella who stayed to see what was going on.

"Dr. Woodard, this is the bank robber and Mr. Simpson's thief all rolled into one," Mandie explained. "He confessed everything to us."

The doctor quickly knelt down to examine the stranger's leg. "It's pretty bad," he said, looking up at Mrs. Taft. "Do you have anywhere we can put this man? Even though he is a criminal he needs medical attention fast."

"Why, yes, I suppose he can be put in an empty room in the servants' quarters. Can you get him upstairs that far? The rooms are on the third floor," Mrs. Taft answered. "He'll be away from us up there."

"We can manage," Dr. Woodard said, standing up.

"We take," Uncle Ned said and motioned for Ben to help him pick up the unconscious man.

They moved slowly up the stairs carrying the criminal. Everyone stood watching. Dr. Woodard followed, giving directions.

"Ella, show them an empty room up there and then bring some coffee and cocoa to the parlor," Mrs. Taft told the maid.

The Negro girl hurried to pass the group on the stairs to direct them to a room.

The young people and Phineas removed their outerwear and left it in the hall and followed Mrs. Taft into the parlor.

Seated by the roaring fire in the parlor the young people related their adventures and Phineas filled in with his as Mrs. Taft listened. Ella brought in hot coffee and hot cocoa and served it.

"The man said his name was Kent Stagrene," Mandie said, pulling the key from her pocket. "I showed him this key that Ben found in the church. He said it belongs to the strongbox he stole from the bank. Then he said somebody else stole the strongbox from him. So I think the man and woman we saw in the church that day must be the ones who robbed him."

Everyone agreed.

Suddenly Mandie caught her breath. "Mr. Phineas!" she said excitedly. "I just happened to remember something. I'm pretty sure the newspaper said there was a reward for the capture of the robber. You can get that money!"

"I didn't capture the robber," Phineas objected. "He captured me. Y'all captured the robber."

Mrs. Taft spoke up quickly. "They're right, Phineas," she said. "You found the man and went after him. Besides, these young people don't need the money. And I'm sure you could use it to get back on your feet."

"Thank you, Mrs. Taft, but I still think they are the ones who actually captured the man," Phineas replied.

"We'll see about that," Mrs. Taft said with a twinkle in her eye.

After a while Dr. Woodard and Uncle Ned joined the others in the parlor.

"Is the robber going to live?" Mandie asked as the two men sat down.

"I think so," the doctor replied. "But he has a bad wound. He should have got medical help right away after it happened. Uncle Ned and Ben filled me in on all the details."

"What are we going to do with him, Dr. Woodard?" Mrs. Taft said uneasily.

"Well, we left Ben watching him for now to make sure he doesn't try to get away if he regains consciousness," the doctor replied. "But we'll have to notify the sheriff that he's here."

"Will the sheriff take him away and put him in jail?" Joe asked.

"I don't think so—not in the condition he's in," his father explained. "I imagine the sheriff will just let him stay here until he is out of danger. Then he'll move him."

"What will they do to him?" Celia inquired.

"That will be up to the bank in Charlotte," Dr. Wood-ard told her. "Our sheriff will probably send him back to the sheriff in Mecklenburg County."

"I never dreamed there would be so much danger," Mrs. Taft said wearily, "or I never would have agreed for these young people to go looking for Mr. Simpson's thief."

Before long, Ella appeared in the doorway to an-nounce that supper was on the table.

In the dining room, they continued discussing the matter as they ate. The young people hardly ate anything, however, because they were too excited. Mrs. Taft said she was too nervous to eat, knowing she had a bank robber in the house. But Phineas, Dr. Woodard, and Uncle Ned made good headway into the delicious food set be-fore them.

Mrs. Taft changed the subject. "How was Hilda when you were up there a while ago?" she asked Dr. Woodard.

"She's just not doing any good," he said, shaking his head.

"Is she conscious?" Mandie asked.

"No, I don't think so," the doctor replied. "She just lies there—doesn't open her eyes or respond in any way."

Ella rushed into the dining room and ran to Mrs. Taft. "De sheriff man he be here," she said. "He want to see you and de doctuh in de parlor."

Mrs. Taft glanced at Dr. Woodard in alarm.

The doctor took charge. "Ella, please tell him we'll be there in a few minutes."

Ella quickly left the room.

"What does he want?" Mrs. Taft asked. "Phineas, you'd better get out of sight. Mr. Simpson may have sent him for you."

Dr. Woodard laid down his napkin and stood up.

"That won't be necessary, Phineas," he said. "We'll just tell him the truth. We have the man upstairs that he's looking for."

Mrs. Taft followed Dr. Woodard out of the room into the parlor. Sheriff Jones was sitting by the fire. He rose to greet them. They all sat down to talk while the young people hid outside the parlor door, watching and listening. Phineas stayed in the dining room.

The sheriff started the conversation. "Sorry to bother you, Mrs. Taft, but—"

"Did that Mr. Simpson send you here?" Mrs. Taft interrupted.

"Well, yes, ma'am, he did," the sheriff admitted. "He told me you have the man who robbed his store, right here in your house."

"Of all the nerve!" Mrs. Taft exclaimed.

"I think I can explain, Sheriff," Dr. Woodard said. "You see, Mr. Simpson thought the man stealing food from his store was a man who is a friend of ours, whom we've known for years. This man's name is Phineas Prattworthy, and he has been living over on the Nantahala Mountain. But it so happens that we know for sure that Phineas is not guilty because we found the man who really stole from Mr. Simpson. He's upstairs. I've just removed a bullet from his leg."

The sheriff looked startled. "A bullet from his leg?" he asked. "Who is this man? Did Mr. Simpson shoot him?"

"No, Mr. Simpson didn't shoot him," the doctor said. "It seems this man also robbed a bank in Charlotte and was shot by a guard."

"That bank robbery last week in Charlotte?" the sheriff asked in disbelief. "You have the man who did it right here in this house?"

"Yes, we do. That's what I've just been telling you," the doctor insisted. "And he's the same man who stole Mr. Simpson's groceries."

The sheriff jumped up. "Where is he? I need to see about moving him to the jail!" he said excitedly.

"It's impossible to move him," the doctor warned. "He let that leg get infected, and right now he's barely hanging on. But if you want to see him, I'll be glad to show you where he is."

"All right," the sheriff agreed.

When the two men made their way up the stairs, the young people came back into the parlor and sat down. Dr. Woodard and the sheriff returned a short time later.

"Are you taking that terrible man out of my house, Sheriff?" Mrs. Taft asked.

The sheriff rubbed his chin thoughtfully. "No, I'm afraid I agree with Dr. Woodard that he shouldn't be moved right now," he said. "Unless you insist that I remove him from the premises, I'll leave him here."

"He can stay here provided someone guards him at all times," Mrs. Taft decided. "I don't want him wandering all over my house."

"He's not able to do any wandering around," Dr. Woodard assured her.

"Well, I can't leave Ben in there to watch him all the time," Mrs. Taft argued. "I need Ben for other things."

"If you'll allow it, I'll send a deputy over to guard him," the sheriff offered.

Mrs. Taft looked relieved. "That will be fine," she said. "Just get him out of my house as soon as it is possible."

At that moment, they heard loud noises outside the house. Everyone looked at each other.

Mandie ran to the window and peeked through the drawn draperies. "Grandmother!" she cried. "There must be a hundred people out in your front yard!"

Mrs. Taft and the sheriff quickly joined her at the window, followed by the others.

"What do they want, Sheriff?" Mrs. Taft asked nervously.

Everyone stared out the window at the sight of people everywhere. Some had lanterns, and they were all screaming something.

The sheriff took charge. "I'll go see what's going on," he said. Heading for the hallway, he opened the front door, and the others followed, staying behind him.

As soon as the door opened, the people on the lawn surged forward. "We want him! We want him!" they cried.

The sheriff took his pistol from its holster and fired a shot into the air. The crowd hushed. His face was in full view in the lamplight from the hallway.

"This is the sheriff here," he told them. "Now, what do you people want?"

"We want that man who desecrated the house of the Lord!" one man cried.

"We want the man who brought all that bad luck to this town with all that bell ringing and writing on the church wall!" a woman yelled.

"Send him out, Sheriff. We're gonna try him here and now!" another man shouted.

"He brung the flu down on this town and caused people to die!" a woman yelled.

The sheriff stepped forward. "Now you wait just a minute!" he hollered. "I'm the law in this town, and we're going to do things by the law as long as I'm sheriff. Now go home—every one of you!"

"We ain't going home till we git that man!" a man insisted.

The angry mob grew louder and louder, pressing closer and closer toward the house. The sheriff raised his gun and fired into the air again.

His shot was answered by another shot from the crowd. "We got guns, too, Sheriff," someone called out. "And we know how to shoot 'em!"

"I'm going to arrest all you troublemakers if you don't move on," the sheriff threatened.

"There ain't a jail big enough to hold us all," a woman yelled.

"Give us that man and we'll leave!" cried a man in front.

"We know you've got him," another bellowed. "Mr. Simpson said so."

Mandie pursed her lips at hearing this. *So Mr. Simpson was the cause of this*, she thought angrily.

"I'm going back inside now," the sheriff called back to the crowd. "We're having supper, and I don't want you moving any closer to this house. I'll discuss the matter with the lady of the house and let you know what she has to say." He quickly closed the door.

Before anyone could say anything, the sheriff turned to Mrs. Taft and explained. "Of course I didn't mean what I told them," he said. "I'm going for help. I left my horse in the backyard. I'll be back as fast as I can. Just don't open the door under any circumstances."

Rushing through the hallway, he headed for the back door. Everyone else looked at each other nervously.

"Let's sit in the parlor," Dr. Woodard suggested, leading the way. "The draperies are all drawn, so they can't see in."

"What are we going to do?" Mrs. Taft asked as they took seats around the room.

"Nothing," Dr. Woodard replied. "We'll just wait for the sheriff to come back."

Everyone sat silently for a few seconds and then Dr. Woodard spoke again. "I need to check on Hilda and our prisoner," he decided. "I won't be long." He stood up and left.

Mrs. Taft also rose. "I think I'll talk to Phineas," she said. "He must still be in the dining room."

"He probably is," Mandie agreed. "We told him to stay there."

When Mrs. Taft left the parlor, Uncle Ned moved

nearer to Mandie. All three young people sat in silence as the noise from the crowd grew stronger.

"They judge," Uncle Ned commented. "Big Book say not judge."

Mandie could feel her anger rising. "That's right, Uncle Ned," she agreed. Suddenly she jumped up and ran to the hallway. "I'm going to tell them what I think of them."

Before anyone could stop her, she opened the door, and the angry mob became very quiet as they saw the door open.

"Please listen to me," Mandie called to the crowd from the front porch. The lamps in the hallway illuminated the area where she stood.

Joe joined her while Uncle Ned and Celia stood back, just inside the house.

When the crowd saw that it was just Mandie, they laughed at her. "Where is the woman of the house?" they yelled. "We don't talk to no young'un!"

Mandie strode to the top of the steps. "Please listen to me!" she yelled at the top of her voice. "I know a lot of you are from our church, and you claim to be Christians. Well, you're not acting Christlike tonight!"

The people nearest the house hushed to listen, and gradually the whole crowd quieted.

"The Bible says, 'Blessed are the merciful; for they shall obtain mercy,'" she reminded them. "You are not showing mercy tonight. You are not behaving at all like Christians."

"Just give us that man," a man yelled. "He's the one who brought all this trouble on our town."

"No, he didn't!" Mandie yelled back. "No human being has the power to bring curses on people, or to cause illness or anything else. You people who are Christians should know that. That's plain old superstition, and there's no place for such thinking in the minds of Christians."

"Just give us that man!" the same man hollered again.

"I want to tell you about the man who was hiding in the church," Mandie continued.

The crowd immediately hushed.

"That man is so poor and disabled that he had to eat out of trash cans," she said. "He had no one left to care whether he lived or died—no one to take care of him." She took a deep breath and went on. "He happened to see a man rush out of Mr. Simpson's store and drop an apple. When he picked it up, Mr. Simpson falsely accused him of stealing. He had done nothing wrong, but he was afraid because he had no one to turn to. He hid in the church, hoping someone would come along who would help him."

"Why didn't he ask somebody to help him?" a woman yelled.

"Because he didn't think he knew anyone in this town," Mandie answered. "He didn't know anyone he could trust. You see, he was living in the Nantahala Mountains with his son. Then his son died, and the man had a stroke and was unable to work. Besides, he's very old."

"Well, Mr. Simpson said he stole from him," a man insisted.

"Tell Mr. Simpson to step forward if he's out there with you," Mandie ordered. "We'll straighten that out right now. Where is Mr. Simpson?"

"He ain't here," a woman said.

"He can't even fight his own battles, is that it?" Mandie mocked. "He has to get the town in an uproar to fight for him?"

"Where is that man who was hiding in the church?" a woman asked.

"He's right here in this house," Mandie replied. "My

grandmother has taken him into her home. Most of you know my grandmother. She would never protect a criminal. You know that."

"How do we know you're telling the truth?" someone yelled.

"Because we also have in this house, and under arrest by the sheriff, the man who *did* steal from Mr. Simpson. He is the same man who robbed the bank in Charlotte. He—"

The crowd went wild. "A bank robber!" they yelled. "In this house?"

Joe moved closer to Mandie and gave her a little pat on the shoulder for encouragement.

"Please let me explain! Please!" Mandie pleaded with the angry crowd.

Finally the people calmed down enough to listen.

"The bank robber was shot at the bank in Charlotte, and we found him out in the woods," Mandie explained. "Dr. Woodard is looking after him, and the sheriff's men are guarding him. As soon as he is able to be moved, he will be put in jail."

An old man stepped forward within the range of the light from the hallway and spoke. "I believe you, little lady. But the man did damage to the house of the Lord, and he ought to be punished for that."

The crowd waited silently for Mandie's reply.

"But that's not for an angry mob to decide," she reminded them. "That's the business of the church members, not the whole town. And not like this."

"I guess you're right, little lady," the old man said. He turned to the crowd. "It's time we'se all in our own homes," he yelled. "Let's go!"

A loud murmuring rippled through the crowd.

"Please go home," Mandie begged. "If you're the Christians you claim to be, you'll go on home. 'Blessed are the merciful; for they shall obtain mercy.' "

One by one, the crowd turned slowly to leave. Mandie's heart was suddenly thumping wildly as she realized what she had done, standing up to this crowd. "Good night, everyone," she called with a slight quiver in her voice. "God bless you."

Several in the crowd repeated her words back to her.

Without turning around, Mandie whispered to Joe, "Joe, I can't move!" she said. "I just realized what I did! They could have mobbed us!"

Joe put his arm around her, gently turning her toward the door. "You sure had me scared to death," he said as they entered the house. "I just knew they were all going to come on into the house!"

Joe closed the door behind them.

Uncle Ned stepped forward, put his arm around Mandie, and led her into the parlor. "Papoose, I proud of you," he said. "Jim Shaw would be proud of Papoose."

Mandie collapsed on the sofa. "Thank you, Uncle Ned," she replied. "Something just came over me, and I had to speak up for Mr. Phineas. I don't know what made me do it."

When Mrs. Taft returned to the parlor with Dr. Woodard and Phineas, they were astounded to hear what had happened.

Mrs. Taft started shaking. "You could have been killed, Amanda!" she exclaimed.

"But she wasn't," Dr. Woodard reminded her. "And she has cleared Phineas's reputation." He smiled at Mandie. "I think you'd make a good lawyer, Amanda—if we had such things as women lawyers."

"No, thank you," Mandie said. "Joe is going to be the lawyer."

Celia stared at her friend in amazement. "I could never have done what you did, Mandie," she said.

By the time the sheriff returned with reinforcements, the crowd had completely dispersed, and all he had to do was leave one deputy to guard the still-unconscious prisoner.

There was no more trouble in the town and Uncle Ned went home.

By the end of the week, Kent Stagrene, the bank robber, had regained consciousness and was well enough to be moved to the jail.

Mandie had kept the key, after showing it to the sheriff.

"I'll just keep it, Sheriff Jones," Mandie told him the day he moved Kent Stagrene from her grandmother's house. "Who knows, I might just find the box it goes to." They were alone in the front hallway.

"What if we find those people? We may need the key," the sheriff said. "Besides, that key belongs to the bank and I think we ought to return it."

"I'll bring it to you in a day or two," she said.

"Miss Amanda, I don't want you getting into any trouble with that key," Sheriff Jones said. "If word got around that you had the key, those gangsters with the strongbox might just come after it."

"But nobody knows I have it except you and my family here," Mandie said. "I promise. I'll bring it to you in a day or two. Please."

The sheriff looked into those blue eyes, so much like those of her mother whom he had once known, and finally smiled and said, "All right. Just a day or two now. Remember, no longer."

As soon as the sheriff left, Mandie hurried to find Joe and Celia. They gathered in the sun room to talk.

"I'm going to have to give up this key," Mandie told them. "What can we do about finding that strongbox before I let the sheriff have this key?"

"Now, Mandie, you are dealing with real gangsters when you try to get involved in this," Joe warned.

"Just tell me where you think they would hide the box," Mandie insisted, ignoring Joe's warning.

Celia spoke up. "Those people may not even be in this town any longer."

"That's right," Joe agreed. "There's no way we could find that box."

"We'll see," Mandie said.

The next morning the sheriff came knocking on the door, asking for Mandie. The adults were all gone and the young people were in the parlor. Ella ushered Sheriff Jones into the room.

"Well, Miss Amanda, I guess I need that key, if you don't mind," the sheriff told her.

"Did you find the box?" Mandie asked eagerly.

"We not only found the box. We also found that man and woman who had stolen it from Kent Stagrene," Sheriff Jones explained.

"Where are they? Can we see them?" Mandie wanted to know.

"Mandie, what do you want to see those people for?" Joe asked impatiently.

"I'd like to see if they're the same people we saw in the church," Mandie said.

"They were," the sheriff confirmed. "They followed Kent Stagrene to his hiding place after he robbed the bank and were able to take the box away from him. They came on into town here with the box with the intentions of staying at the hotel. When they went to register, the hotel clerk saw the box and recognized it as a bank box."

"Why didn't the clerk have them arrested?" Mandie asked.

"Well, instead of notifying my office the clerk thought he could get a reward for himself and he asked the strangers if they wanted to put their money box in the safe. The people suddenly decided they didn't want to register and left. The clerk followed them. The man and woman split up. The clerk tried to keep up with the man but the man was too smart for him. And the woman completely disappeared."

"You still haven't said how you know they were in the church," Mandie insisted.

"When we caught them they said they had lost the key in the church," the sheriff explained.

"Now we know," Celia said with a sigh.

"Where were they from, Sheriff Jones?" Mandie asked.

"No place in particular," the sheriff said. "They are professional gamblers and they travel from place to place, wherever they can set up games. They just happened to be in the bank when Kent Stagrene robbed it."

"Thanks for letting me know, Sheriff," Mandie said. "And, Sheriff, would you please do me a favor? Would you give the bank Mr. Phineas Prattworthy's name as the one who captured the robber? I understand the reward offered was for capture of the robber. And Mr. Phineas needs the reward money real bad."

"There are two rewards offered, one for the man and another one for the money," the sheriff explained. "As officers of the law we can't collect rewards so we'll just turn in his name for both rewards. I'm sure he'll be hearing from the bank."

"What about the hotel clerk?" Joe asked.

"He didn't capture the money," the sheriff said. "My deputy happened to be right there when it happened and he took the money box from the people."

"Thank you, Sheriff Jones. The rewards will mean so much to Mr. Phineas," Mandie said, smiling at the law officer.

And in a few days the bank in Charlotte sent a special messenger to see Phineas Prattworthy, bringing a letter of thanks and an enormous reward.

"I still don't feel I deserve it," the old man declared as they all sat in the parlor after the messenger left. "But I do owe the church for damages because of my bad conduct."

"You'll have plenty for that and plenty left over to live on," Mrs. Taft replied.

"Thank the Lord," Mandie said softly.

Mrs. Taft offered Phineas a house and farm that she owned near Asheville. He could make a good living off it with the help of a few hired hands which he could now afford. He was thankful for her kindness.

The next Saturday Uncle Cal came by Mrs. Taft's house with the message that classes would resume on the following Monday.

"I'm glad to see you, Uncle Cal," Mandie told the old Negro as she and Celia stood talking to him in the front hallway, "but I was hoping we'd have a little longer out of school."

"But, Missy, all dem girls done got well now, and you gotta keep on wid dat book learnin' so you won't be ignorant," he teased.

"Aren't you coming in?" Celia invited.

"No, Missy. I got lots of calls to make to git the girls all back to school," he replied, thanking her. "But me and Phoebe, we see y'all come Monday." And with that he left.

Mandie closed the door and turned toward the parlor. "Oh, shucks!" she said.

"But, Mandie, we knew everyone was better when Dr. Woodard told us he and Joe were going home yesterday," Celia reminded her.

They both sat down near the fireplace in the parlor.

"I know," Mandie said with a sigh. "Oh, well, the house seems so empty with everyone else gone that I suppose we might as well go back to school. And we do still have a mystery back there to solve. Remember our little problems with a certain mouse?" she asked.

Celia nodded. "Oh, yes," she said. "We never did get that cleared up, did we?"

Mandie sat silently for a minute. "I just wish Hilda would get well." She sighed again.

"At least when Dr. Woodard went home, he said she was no worse," Celia reminded her. "And he has those nurses staying with her around the clock. Maybe she'll change for the better soon."

Just then there was a knock on the door, and Mandie rushed to answer it.

When she opened the door, there stood Uncle Ned, smiling down at her. "Uncle Ned, come on in," Mandie greeted the old Indian, ushering him into the parlor. "I didn't know you were coming back so soon."

"I bring message from mother of Papoose," he said, sitting by the fire to warm his hands. He smiled broadly.

Snowball, who was curled up on the rug nearby, opened one eye to look at him and then went back to sleep.

"Good news?" Mandie asked excitedly.

"Yes. Good News," the Indian replied. "Mother of Papoose say she have big surprise for Papoose for Christmas."

"Surprise for Christmas?" Mandie puzzled over the message. "Tell me what it is, Uncle Ned. Please?"

"Not know, Papoose," Uncle Ned told her. "Mother of Papoose say she not tell me so I not tell Papoose."

"You mean Mother sent you all the way over here to tell me she had a big surprise for me for Christmas, and she didn't even tell you what it is?" Mandie frowned.

"I not know surprise, Papoose," the Indian repeated.

"Not even a little teeny bit?" Mandie teased.

Uncle Ned reached over to her and patted her blonde head. "Papoose, I not know surprise. Must wait for Christmas," he said with a smile.

"Oh, no," Mandie moaned. "I'll be wondering from now until Christmas holidays what this is all about."

"So will I," Celia added.

"It must be something awfully important for her to send you, Uncle Ned," Mandie reasoned.

The old Indian grinned. "Papoose see," he said. "Wait for Christmas."

After Uncle Ned left that afternoon, Mandie paced up and down in the parlor talking through this newest mystery. Celia sat patiently by the fire, petting Snowball.

What surprise could her mother have for her that was important enough to send Uncle Ned with the message? Mandie wondered. And why didn't her mother just wait until Mandie came home for the holidays and tell her about the surprise then?

Mandie could hardly wait.